PROSE FICTION

PROSE FICTION

*UEA MA
Creative Writing Anthologies
2021*

CONTENTS

AYÒBÁMI ADÉBÁYÒ Foreword		VII
PHILIP LANGESKOV & TESSA MCWATT Introduction		IX
OPE ADEDEJI Abnormal Boy		2
SINDRE AMUNDSEN Mors		8
TRISHA ANDRES The Procession		12
WILL BINDLOSS Jolt		18
HANNAH COLE Win Her Back Wednesdays		24
CONOR DUGGAN The Egg and the Skipping Rope		32
ISABEL EDAIN Moth & Meredith		38
POLLY HALLADAY She Visits		44
MYRIAL A HOLBROOK The Land Is Darkened		50
ADAM HUSAIN Every Word of This is True		56
SHEREEN JACKSON Everything is Fine		62
NOZIZWE CYNTHIA JELE Platinum Tupperware		68
ROSE KEATING Eggshells		74
DEREK KEOGH The Will		82
TAWSEEF KHAN Leave To Remain		88
LILLIE LAINOFF The Mustard Children		94
MICHELE LIM Wandering Point		100
OLIVIA LOWDEN Salvation Army		108
MAX LURY The Dutchman		114
JAMES MILDREN Easter Sunday		122
ADEOLA OPEYEMI Of Home and Other Places We Claim		128
VICTORIA OSBORN 5831. Tishrei *and* Present Tense		134
JONATHAN PADWAY Negatives		142
ARIANE PARRY A Comedian		148
HELEN RYE Two flash fictions: The Lost Girls and Reel		154
TWISHAA TANDON Mirabai		158
ROSE VAN ORDEN Chimera Forever		164
ALASTAIR WONG Gesamtkunstwerk; Total Work of Art		170
KATHERINE YONG YHAP Tale One		176
Acknowledgements		183

AYỌ̀BÁMI ADÉBÁYỌ̀
Foreword

Suzanne Ushie was supposed to be my classmate, but she preceded me to Norwich by a year. Though we both lived in Nigeria, we had never met in person, only becoming acquainted when we learnt that we were to start UEA's MA in Prose Fiction at the same time. We stayed in touch as September approached, looking forward to our time together at UEA as the only Nigerians in that year's cohort. Then we applied for our visas. Suzanne got hers but my application was denied, forcing me to defer my admission for another year.

We continued to check in via email, sharing links to opportunities, chatting about her unfolding year and my preparations to resume later. Through her I arrived on the programme before I enrolled, living vicariously through our correspondence, her words a window into the life that could soon be mine. At some point we began to share our writing. First, links to what we had published, then early drafts we had not pitched to any publications yet.

Suzanne had already flown back to Lagos when I eventually landed in Norwich. However, she had left gifts for me in the care of someone in her cohort, who had stayed on to pursue a doctorate. Within days of my arrival, the items – an iron, a water filter, an electric kettle, bed sheets, sweaters, winter jackets, coursework materials – had been delivered to me. And though I had never met Suzanne in person, her generosity would cushion my first few months at UEA. The lack of an opportunity for a physical meeting did not make our kinship less vital. Instead, it seemed to clarify how all we already shared – a love for books, an almost compulsive desire to write, gratitude for the great gift of a year spent thinking, reading, and writing – could transcend distance.

From the beginning of their MA year, the cohort published here has had to devise ways to replicate for themselves a simulacrum of community as the world went in and out of lockdowns. Where some alumni will fondly remember the ritual of fraternising in the grad bar after workshops, this class studied while at a remove from each other for lengths of time. What they have lost or gained because of these unusual circumstances cannot yet be measured and may well be beyond quantification.

The stories and excerpts here display the thrilling promise that earned these writers their place on the programme. They also herald the ascent of future literary stars. A man mourns his beloved as he works his way through a checklist. An immigration lawyer tries to help a client who is in trouble. In London, a waiter watches ghosts mill around the changed city. While in Lagos, a mother can no longer wait for her son to die like her previous children have. Loss rips through the anthology in various forms, echoing the grief-laced year the Covid-19 pandemic has brought upon many countries.

Perhaps this through-line is indicative of how, like Suzanne and me, these writers have happened upon the gift of intellectual companionship that flourishes even when there is no opportunity to spend hours together in the same seminar rooms. It is possible to speculate then, that while they may not have put in hours at the grad bar, this cohort is leaving Norwich with something else alumnae often speak of with gratitude about the MA year – the discovery of writers whose opinions they will continue to value and treasure for years to come.

PHILIP LANGESKOV & TESSA MCWATT
Introduction

We are writing these words in late May. I am in a small, commandeered room in my house in Norwich. Tessa is at her desk that looks out over the rooftops of Kilburn, in London. I am wearing two T-shirts, a shirt and a thick winter cardigan. Although it's hard to be certain – Teams is being glitchy at present – I'd say Tessa is wearing something similar, certainly a jumper, pretty thick by the looks of things. It is late May – did we mention? AccuWeather™ says that this period of heavy rain will continue for more than 60 minutes. The temperature is 10° C. The RealFeel™, staggeringly, is 5° C. It is late May – did we mention? Tomorrow, we will be meeting up with our students – the writers with whom we began working in September, the writers whose words you are about to read – for the very first time in person. It is late May – did we mention?

In more normal circumstances, we would both be in our offices on the UEA campus. In more normal circumstances it would probably be between 13° and 17° C, with the RealFeel™ perhaps a notch or two higher even than that; it gets muggy in Norfolk around now. In more normal circumstances we would not be meeting our students for the first time in person in late May. In more normal circumstances we would not have become so used to writing the words 'in more normal circumstances'. You get the picture. This is 2021, pandemic year, the year in which the strange became punishingly familiar, and the familiar alluringly strange. Nothing – weather, dress, contact – has been as it should have been. Viktor Shklovsky would have had a field day.

When the first lockdown came – back in March 2020 – there was a good deal of heated talk about the effect of lockdown on writers, about the ways in which the discombobulation and anxiety occasioned by this new way of living might find its way into their work, both in terms of practice and output. It was said, frequently, that writers would never have a better opportunity to write – 'Look,' the people saying these things appeared to be saying, 'at all the *time* you have at your disposal. Get on with it!' It was also said, with almost equal frequency, that it was hard to imagine a time *less* conducive to writing – people were dying, after all, in their hundreds of thousands; livelihoods, already precarious, were very widely under threat; governing classes the world over were found wanting to a very surprising degree. At the same time, we heard stories of people turning to books in unprecedented numbers, of local independent booksellers laying on home deliveries, becoming first responders to a nation in troubled isolation.

In the midst of all this – as lockdowns were eased, then reimposed; as R-numbers went down and then, alarmingly, up – nearly fifty writers 'arrived' in Norwich to take part in the MA Prose Fiction at UEA, a programme of study that was about to celebrate its fiftieth anniversary – the oldest such course in the United Kingdom and one of the oldest in the world. They weren't to know it, but they would form the largest cohort of writers we have ever had. (There is useful research to be done into the reasons why so many people, not only here, chose, in a time of crisis, to turn towards art. Research that could usefully be read by any number of governments who seem determined to make the practice of art a luxury and a privilege). None of us knew at the time that not only would the course begin online, but that it would remain so, almost without exception, for the duration of the academic year. Until now, in fact, until this week in late May. And so, those writers – from all over the world – found themselves in a new city from which they were exiled. Similar experiences were had all over the world, many of them considerably worse. We know that, but nonetheless we feel for the writers in this volume, who came all this way for an experience that was considerably outside the realm of the usual. We salute them as well, for their fierce determination to keep writing and to take care, both of themselves and their fellow writers. We feel, too, for the writer who should have been in this volume, had it not been for a coup in their home country that prevented them from returning here in January. We hope that they are able to read these words, that they and their loved ones are safe; we hope, too, that they will be able to join us again in September, to finish what they started.

And, nevertheless, in and amongst *all this*, there was art: short stories, novel extracts, flash fiction, all of which belie that exile, that lay out real and imagined worlds against the pause of lockdown, against hopelessness. You will find that art in this volume, among familiar and unfamiliar things. There are love stories and break-up stories; there are stories of homecoming, stories of departure; there are stories that defy such means of accounting. They are not about this strange year, not exactly, but they have emerged out of it and so constitute a record of some sort, a series of acts of witness. Over the fifty years of this programme, many very fine writers have passed through its workshops and seminars and dissertation supervisions. There are twenty-nine more in this book, each with something to say, each with a story to tell. All of them are deserving of your attention. Tomorrow, if AccuWeather™ is to be believed, the sun will come out and the temperature, at last, will begin to rise. Tomorrow, for the first time, we will meet these writers in the flesh, the same writers that you are about to meet on the page. Here's to them and here's to tomorrow.

Philip Langeskov & Tesssa McWatt
May 2021

This diverse anthology comprises the latest work from the 2021 cohort of prose writers studying UEA's renowned Creative Writing MA.

OPE ADEDEJI

Ope Adedeji is a writer and editor from Lagos, Nigeria. She's the 2020 Booker Prize Scholar at the University of East Anglia. Her work has appeared in *McSweeney's Quarterly*, *Catapult*, *Lolwe*, *Masters Review* and so much more. She sends a weekly newsletter on ope.substack.com.

@Opeadedeji_
opeadedeji95@gmail.com

Abnormal Boy
A short story

Your boy will leave today. You're sure of it before his teacher calls. You shut your laptop and begin chewing the skin of your thumb. You move to the nail, biting the grime in the corners, then chipping the edge off.

The date is marked on your calendar app: 'April 6, 2021 – Bobo is leaving today.' A mother knows these things. You saw it the day you pushed him out at the Catholic hospital – a warm day six years ago – and a white nurse placed his cool skin against the streaks of sweat on your chest. You knew that despite your prayers to Jesus in Shiloh or the female goat you sacrificed to Ọṣun, that this boy would leave you, the way the others before him did, the way his father did.

Was that a smile you saw?

The nurse chuckled as she tucked the covers around your abdomen. 'Newborn babies can't smile.'

But what about this scar on his neck? Where did it come from?

The nurse fingered it, a frown creasing her forehead. 'It's only a birthmark.' Her laughter was dry and hollow. It rings in your ears now as you tie your shoelace.

Your feet vibrate in your shoes as you paint red lipstick on trembling lips. It slips down to the hairs beneath your chin. Your hands are shaking. This fear is not new. It's always with you, especially when he threatens you with raging fevers. It starts in your chest, sitting in both breasts and sternum before heating the back of your neck and shaking your thighs and feet.

It's time.

All morning, you held on to your rosary, muttering 'Hail Mary, full of grace' and staring at your phone's lock screen – a picture of him with a 'fro, cutting his *Black Panther* cake on his fifth birthday. You were unable to work because you knew.

A mother always knows.

The classroom smells of crayons.

Your boy sits in the corner of the buzzing room, flipping through a newspaper. His nose doesn't seem to be runny, and he doesn't look tired, so you are perplexed. If he isn't sick, why has Ms Okereke called you to come right away? He doesn't raise his gaze to you. His thin legs are drawn up to his chest. They have spiral lines on them, probably from scratching the bumps of mosquito bites with a pencil.

The first time you had a baby, you and Bobo had been new lovers. He had a tattoo of your name on his clavicle. You had one of *Star Wars*, his favourite movie, on your waist. It was a rainy season, and every morning, he brought you snails, freshly picked from the wet garden and cooked in tomato sauce. In between Skype meetings, he'd jump into the messy sheets, place his head on your navel to listen for the baby's kicking. His cat-shaped eyes held light in them, even on nights he didn't sleep because you were uncomfortable. The baby – you named him Joy – died in his sleep two days before his first birthday, and Bobo smashed bottles of essential oils he bought you against the wall. He cried; you didn't.

You pluck a strand of hair beneath your chin as you wait for your boy to notice you. It's now closing time, and the class is emptying. Little boys in oversized white shirts stand around their tables in groups. They arrange colouring books into their desks, zip their bags. A boy runs to his mother, standing at the door to the classroom. If your boy were like every other boy, he would run to you.

'Your boy is something,' Ms Okereke says, lightly touching your arm. Her voice is clogged with phlegm.

She comes over to stand by your side and stares at him through hidden eyes. She slips her fingers into the pocket of her dusty grey coat.

You nod. 'What happened?'

She folds her lips till they touch the tip of her nose.

'He's been in the corner since morning, refusing to eat or participate.' She claps her hands, then presses your shoulder, bringing her lips to your ears. 'There's a problem. This is the same thing he did yesterday and on Monday. You must take him somewhere where they can figure out the problem. Would you try Shiloh?'

You cough, your acrylic nails firmly pinching the corner of your jaw where a clump of hair sits. You thank her and go on to bundle him in your arms.

On your way home, he tells you he's going soon. He sits on your lap at the back of a keke napep that slowly snakes through traffic. Vendors selling yoghurts, sausage rolls and plantain chips walk past. Normal children would ask their mothers to buy for them. Not your boy.

'You know that place I'm going to? I can't wait to get there,' he says, drumming his lips. 'Before I came here, we used to sing and dance there.'

You know who 'we' is – your dead children: Joy and Banjoko. You press him into your chest, and turn his face to yours. His uniform is damp with sweat, woolly to touch. In his brown squinted eyes is a vacant stare. This is what you get for going to Shiloh to pray for a child, then carry that same belly to Ọṣun for her blessings. A boy who is torn in his spirit. Your eyes brim with tears.

He suddenly looks at you through wide brown eyes as though listening to your thoughts. He giggles. 'Mummy, are you crying?' His face is his father's. You wipe your eyes and stare into the sun. There's a sharp pain in your chest.

The second time you had a baby, she stayed only long enough for you to give her a name. You called her Banjoko, after an aunt that you loved when you were a girl. Different hands carried her that evening as your family celebrated, breaking kola nuts and drinking beer. By 10 p.m., when everyone had gone to their homes, baby Banjoko began crying. It started as a whimper and grew till it was so loud, the neighbours complained. She was burning with a fever. Sitting naked by her crib, you forced your nipple into her mouth, refusing to allow Bobo to take her to the hospital. You knew there was no point. She would leave too.

At midnight, she was dead.

Bobo collapsed on you, pressing his body into your face, suffocating you. Under his weight, you dug your nails into baby Banjoko's neck and, before the ambulance arrived, you burnt the mark your nails made on her neck with a lighter and watched the leaf-shaped darkness spread. Bobo screamed 'madness'. The house smelled of incense.

The plump woman next to you pulls your boy's cheeks. 'What a good boy,' she says, digging through her bag.

Your boy's face crumples together and smoothes out before he begins to scream. His eyes are red, and there are green veins on his temples. The woman hands him kopiko candy, but he throws it at her, his screams piercing the hot afternoon.

You face the woman with pleading eyes.

'I'm sorry. I'm sorry,' she says, her voice hoarse.

You rub your boy's chest and whisper 'good boy' several times into his ears. He's not a good boy; he's a bad boy.

You ask him if he can be a normal boy. He laughs. It's the laughter of an old man playing ayo and drinking beer at noon. He squeezes your fingers, stares into your eyes, shakes his head.

'I'm going soon,' he says.

You both watch the news at nine. He comments 'rubbish' when a pastor claims he has the cure for corruption.

Where do children pick up these things? Probably from the other children that came before him. Joy and Banjoko. Your mother thinks children like him, like Joy and Banjoko, have meetings at night when you're asleep, meetings where they come up with new ways to haunt you. You slap your thighs to shake away the thoughts. You shouldn't think like your mother.

Next to you on a side stool is the dented bottle of holy water you got from Shiloh. There's also the crucifix of Jesus and the Ọṣun statue you ordered on Amazon. You want to attempt to keep him here with you, but you know he won't stay. In the past year, you went from doctor to doctor, asking for an explanation. They prised your legs open, took blood from your boy, asked for sample stool, examined his eyes, then your mouth.

There was no explanation, nothing to explain the two dead children that chased the love of your life away. He said the dreams of dead babies were too much for him. You asked, what about my body? He said your body was cursed.

You shut your eyes. There's solace in darkness; it's sweet and sour like agbalumo seeds. Your mind roams the darkness. First, you're in the delivery room, screaming at the nurse to push the boy back into your vagina. Then you're in the toilet shitting slippery shit, and the boy is in front of you, laughing. By the time you open your eyes, the power has gone off. Your eyes stretch in the darkness. They caress the rough, cream walls and draw a straight line until it reaches the sofa on which the boy had been sitting. Has he left you already?

In the room, you watch him sleep. His arms are frail, and his lips pouted. His pyjamas are made from silk and have lilac flower patterns. Saliva oozes through his slightly parted lips.

Anytime now.

That he's stayed this long has sometimes deceived you into believing that he would stay forever, but you've never been an optimistic person. You blame yourself for the misfortune. Six years ago, excited that the start-up you worked for had just gotten some funding, thanks to the pitch decks you made, you called Bobo to celebrate with you.

'What the hell, why not?' He said.

When he arrived, he had bottles of red wine and cans of beer. You smelled of strawberries. The kisses started at the screen door, ushering mosquitoes in. It didn't take long before he was biting your neck, your navel, your thighs. He was gone before morning. No notes, just the boy he dumped inside you.

You were going to keep the boy, you told your mother when asked. She held her tongue, refusing to say it would end in tears. She knew as mothers know. She took you to Shiloh first, then to Ọṣun's river. You fasted, prayed, declared. He would stay. You told Bobo he would survive. You told him to come back to you. Maybe the other babies died because you didn't get married in a church. You would have a church wedding and wear a white dress. The baby would stay. He stopped picking up your calls.

When the boy came, whatever hope you had evaporated. The scar on his neck was proof. You knew, just as you know now. So you didn't name him. He'd be known as Boy. A boy after his father.

A gecko zips at a cockroach above the wide-open curtains that bring in the moon. The boy snores and twists, one leg angled towards the wall, the other on the edge of the bed. He sucks on his thumb.

You rewrap your wrapper and climb into bed with him. The bed creaks as you lay flat on him. He stirs beneath you. He's warm. You wrap your hands around his neck, pushing yourself into him. His eyes fly open. Yours brim with tears. Your body quakes. You hear grumbling, the start of a scream. You clasp tighter, shrinking the sheets, sinking the bed. He kicks the air.

'Mummy, please. I won't do that again.' His voice is muffled.

You don't stop even when he becomes limp and cold.

In the morning, twisting the hairs under your chin, you call his teacher. 'Boy won't be in today.' Then you call Bobo to tell him the news.

SINDRE AMUNDSEN

Sindre Amundsen grew up near Oslo, in Norway. After serving conscription, he worked as a hospital porter. He later studied English in Kristiansand. There he began writing fiction, and went to study creative writing in York. He returned to Oslo to study English Literature, before applying to the Prose MA at UEA, and now resides in Norwich.

sindre_am@hotmail.com

Mors
An excerpt from a novel

MORS. It was written in capital letters across the screen of the oval, blue and rubber-edged device that Lars held in his hand. For every button-press, it buzzed forcefully, twice. It sounded like an angry wasp stuck in his chest pocket. The square screen lit up, and displayed a location, a birth date, a room, as well as the requisitioner's name. When the calling said MORS, he had to copy the job to send it to a colleague and wait.

Lars stood waiting with his hands behind his back towards the wall and looked down the long corridor where young nurses were zooming between rooms like bees in a flower bed. He looked at the legs of the attractive ones who wore tight white scrubs. One of them came over to him and asked by pointing to the room with raised brows and he said he was waiting for his colleague. She went away and he wondered if he had acted attractively. He fidgeted with the calling and looked at the birth date again. 89 was too close to his own. He started wandering back and forth in the corridor. The birth date said a lot about what his trip with a patient would be like, even when they were just going to an X-ray. If it ended in 25–30, they could be boringly nice, dull, or basically dead already. Anything from late 80s to early 90s he felt himself expanding and tried shaping himself into something cool, detached, and appealing in case it was somebody he liked. Which department the job came from mattered too. The H-shaped hospital building stretched like an odd body downwards. At the top, brain stuff. Near the bottom, gyn and births. Finally, the basement was for rubbish, dead bodies, and the kitchen.

Lars heard the mechanical doors open and saw Charles carrying the rectangular steel plate (to keep it from getting lost) with the key to the morgue. Lars opened the large door to room 506 for him. Charles's wispy grey hair tried to escape his scalp as he strode along with clenched bum cheeks. His back pocket carried a black comb he used to wet in the sink to drag the wild strands of hair down to the side, and his glasses gave him a bug-eyed look. He was among the speediest of his colleagues. He was the only Englishman working there, and his wife was a CEO of some sports company. Lars followed him into the room. When he entered a MORS-room, Lars expected certain smells, a gloomy scene. But that was never the case. He saw Charles signing the morgue document, as sunlight through the window from across the green valley played with the warm quiet dust and blinked in the glass vase of pink roses. The room was tidy, containing nothing but the moveable drawer that the flowers were on, the bed, and the body underneath a sheet, the outline of which looked nothing like a person trying to hide, for instance. He wondered what people were seeing as they wheeled the body out into the elevator hall, where visitors came out from the smaller lifts. Lumps of bedding? Charles had pressed the big ↓ button and held his hand on his hip as he stood against the wall. He smiled at Lars. 'Går det bra?' he asked in a thick accent.

'Yup,' Lars said and nodded.

He felt crowded inside the lift. He had to shuffle in beside the bed to make room for Charles by the door. They were quiet, necks taut as they were looking down. It stopped on the third floor, where light and the smell of floor cleaner engulfed them. A surgeon stepped away from the doors, jogged away to their left, and they heard him opening the flimsy door to the staircase instead. The door stayed open for a little while, 00:01_00:02_00:03_00:04 and closed. They were in the dim and dull metal box again. The presence of something beyond the two of them was palpable in the silence, and Lars felt the air had taken on a thickness, things floating in it.

The doors opened to the red floor in front of the clear plastic flaps to the kitchen, and Lars pulled the bed out as Charles went ahead. To the left, a metal door separated the new hospital from the old new-baroque building, used only for offices, drug rehabilitation day centres, and a morgue. The automatic door-opener whirred behind them and the lights were zapping on in flashes too slowly. Lars had to steer the bed clear of the procession of broken ones lining the wall. Some of them were rusted, others stripped bare, scavenged for parts. As Lars turned the corner, Charles stood at the end of the corridor holding another white door open, knuckle on his hip. Together they pushed the bed into the cold room where large black ceiling fans droned. Toes stuck out beneath sheets on a thin steel shelf. The air smelled sterile, and the cold filled his lungs like cotton. To the right of the entry, names were pinned on a noticeboard in a grid matching the shelves where they lay.

They lined up the steel stretcher alongside the bed before locking it into place. Lars pulled down the top sheet, making sure he didn't touch the body, although he would have to in a minute. Their hands felt for a firm grip of the top of the next sheet, which the body was wrapped in. It was held in place by two safety pins at the top. Sometimes it came apart, and Lars swore that he had once seen purple eyes looking up at him. But treating the body as not a body at all, but a person asleep, was part of what Charles had taught him. Charles never made a big deal of it, rarely talked about it afterwards, except to scrunch his nose up and say he didn't like that part of the job. They had a grip on the sheet and felt the warmth escape from underneath the body as they lifted it to the steel stretcher, and they grew quiet, as grave robbers do. They could tell it was a woman, by size and weight. But they did not think as much. It seemed too vast a space for thoughts. Like the hairdresser's chair, the foot pedal of the stretcher lifted or sank the body, and depending on the weight, it would wobble. They aligned the stretcher to the shelf perfectly to make sure it wouldn't slide off and crash.

They pushed it into place, all the way against the wall until it stuck in a groove. The bed had to be delivered for cleaning, and Charles patted Lars on the back as if saying thanks before he'd even agreed to do it and ran up a side stair to the offices above. As Lars stood next to the bed in the large elevator, he too felt kind of empty, and the bright white sheet left on the bed seemed too loud to him. He borrowed a pen and some paper from a nurse on the fifth floor, steered the bed into the east wing washroom, wrote 'Mors' on the note and placed it on the bed.

Lars glanced at the grey screen, but there was no new job. He walked out into the elevator hall, when he heard the ding of one arriving, voices inside and echoing. When the door opened, he recognised Anna's long blonde hair as she was pulling the bed out onto the floor. She smiled as she saw him, but kept talking to the patient, a small elderly lady with chalk white hair. Lars stood by the door to the stairs as he watched Anna's ponytail dance against her back when she pressed the lever by the door. He saw her plant her feet in the ground and engage her hips as she turned the bed to the left, into room 506. There the sun would still be coming through the window over the over-green trees, the dust particles would mimic the noise inside shut eyelids, and someone would have replaced the pink roses with daffodils and a glass of water.

TRISHA ANDRES

Trisha Andres is a journalist and broadcaster. Most recently, she was Commissioning Editor for Travel at the *Daily Telegraph*, commissioning writers including Orhan Pamuk and Naomi Alderman. Trisha has written for the *Financial Times*, *The Guardian* and *Condé Nast Traveller*. She grew up in the Philippines, the US and the UK. Her fiction explores identity, place and what it means to belong.

trisha.andres@gmail.com
trishaandres.com
twitter.com/trisha_andres

The Procession
An extract from a novel centred on two women's search for independence and identity amidst the confines of privilege and duty, set in 1980s Philippines under the Marcos regime.

CHAPTER 14

Ghost pipefish and oriental sweetlips leapt from the water, alongside our boat. The island ahead was an immodest green, palms smothering the fringes. But no one took any notice. Lola Rosa's voice drowned out the breaking of the waves and the revving of the motor.

'Maya, please put some sunblock on your neck? You're going to get so dark.'

'Did we have to bring her along?' Maya asked me.

'I can hear you, you know.' Lola Rosa said.

'Morena is beautiful too; it's all the rage in Europe. Don't worry about Maya getting darker,' I said. But what was the point of debating with Lola Rosa? I'd never convince her that centuries of colonialism had brainwashed her into thinking we were an inferior race. She insisted the only way to remedy this flaw was to slather on Pond's whitening cream. Next to me, a woman in a striped yellow dress spread sunscreen on her legs like clotted cream on a scone.

I had no plan. I just knew we had to get to the hospital in El Nido Town – even if that meant bringing Lola Rosa along. She had insisted on accompanying us. We didn't need a chaperone. But she'd argued she had friends in high places at the hospital. I was too desperate to find my grandmother to interrogate what that actually meant.

The day was humid. Monsoon season had come and gone, which left howling wind and sunshine so exuberant it verged on controversial.

'It's so hot,' a man said, as if revealing a secret. The couple next to us discussed the upcoming elections. It was getting heated. The wife, who was wearing short shorts, threatened to cut off the man's penis if he voted for Marcos. Maya sniggered.

'Oh, ikaw bata ka, I heard from Josie you got arrested.' Lola Rosa turned to Maya.

'Do you really need to bring that up now?' Maya said.

'Why are you so against Marcos? He built all these beautiful buildings, fed poor people, and he's a great ambassador for the country. Look at all the presidents he's friends with: Nixon, Gaddafi, Chairman Mao. We wouldn't be so famous around the world if it weren't for him.'

Maya turned red. 'Famous around the world...'

I kicked her shin, but Maya was undeterred.

'Famous around the world? For what? For killing hundreds of construction workers because his wife wanted to get the Centre for Film finished in time for Miss Universe? Miss Universe!'

A mother in a black-skirted swimsuit covered her son's sunburnt ears with her hands. Glaring at Maya, the arguing couple scuttled away from us.

'What are you looking at?' Lola Rosa said, with the reckless rage she reserved for swatting flies in the kitchen.

I wondered what my own grandmother was like. I hadn't considered a second granny, content with the one I'd known all my life, who wore red lipstick and silk shirts that smelt of bergamot and pink peppercorn, who was a daring documentarian of the world. This new grandma would be different, I was sure; but in what way? Would she be like Lola Rosa, welcoming me into her home and feeding me to bursting point? I hadn't considered what I would do if she turned me away. Lola Rosa put her dainty, manicured feet on the wooden bench opposite her. Her cornflower nail varnish was the same shade of blue as the makeshift footstool.

We soon disembarked, with Maya and me trailing after Lola Rosa, who was using her umbrella as a cane. She opened the brolly, the size of a gazebo, printed with balloon patterns.

'What the—' Maya began.

'Maya, your mouth,' Lola Rosa said.

'What do we need the umbrella for?' I asked.

'It's for the two of you, especially you.' She narrowed her eyes at Maya.

'Let me do that, Lola Rosa.' I took the umbrella from her.

'You're sweet, hija, but it's the two of you we need to shield from the sun, not me. I'm old, and in any case, my skin's wrinkled like a fisherman's. There's no hope for me. But the two of you...'

Maya forged ahead in a huff, leaving me behind with Lola Rosa and an umbrella straight out of *My Fair Lady*. I passed it back to her, my eyes issuing an apology. We jogged along the jetty. Three boys in white sacristan outfits hurried past us. We made a right after Jarace Grill on Rizal Street and were met with a human traffic jam of sweaty bodies.

I was pressed next to a man so close I could feel the pineapple fabric of his shirt against my arm. 'What's going on?' I asked him.

'It's the Santacruzan,' he said, before navigating the crowd like a ballroom dancer.

Lola Rosa, Maya and I huddled together. I took Lola Rosa's hand and she took Maya's. We followed the man's lead, spinning and twirling between people: a tourist in a red bikini top and denim shorts so tight they looked like they'd cut off her circulation; a fisherman in cargo shorts and a white T-shirt with San Miguel written across it; and the same group of young sacristans trying to free themselves from the gridlock. At the bottom of the street was the church. Hurtling towards us was a precarious train of Virgin Marys. The first was a Mother Mary draped in pink with flowers at her feet, the next a classic blue and white Virgin Mary with a lace platform on wheels.

I didn't agree with the idea of young women dressed in silk and lace to celebrate the coming of the rains, as if they were sacrificial offerings to God, but I adored a Santacruzan. Hadn't Bobby told me my birth mother had been a Reyna Elena when she was younger? I imagined her smiling in an understated dress, unlike the tiered cake constructions of the other gowns on show. I wondered what my grandmother thought of the pageant. I hoped she'd recognise me.

The sky was getting dark. Stars on the cusp of making an appearance. Lola Rosa clapped to the music: a soft murmur – was it church music? – before it grew louder, vociferous, leaving the choir's lips, escaping into the late afternoon. We had no choice but to follow the procession. Overtaking a cargo bike carrying three statues of the Santo Niño, we joined the tail end of the queue, right behind the giant crucifix, which stood tall and proud like a decorated war veteran. The young men carrying it above their heads hobbled as if wounded. Couldn't they move any faster?

'I would've loved to join,' Maya said.

'And prance around like that?' I pointed at a woman in a purple embellished dress with a hoop skirt twice her girth.

'Why not? I'm a queen,' Maya said.

'Yes, you are,' I said, but now was not the time for daydreaming. 'Can we get to the hospital any quicker?'

'There's no other way than through the streets they're taking.' Maya gestured at the crowd.

The organisers lit the candles one by one, until the whole procession was sheathed in light. The queens and their gowns came to life. A Reyna turned around to adjust her dress. I suppressed a scream. Her face was caked in ghoulish foundation. Past the Reyna Elena was a small boy dressed as a little prince in miniature satin garments, topped with a golden paper crown. Past him was a cordoned-off street. Behind the ropes were rows of long tables covered with bright flowered oilcloth, illuminated by streetlamp posts. We teetered closer. Fruit flies whirred around cling film-wrapped plates of pancit bihon and red hotdogs. There was also puto, a staple of any self-respecting festival, and sugared spaghetti. On one corner of the street was a man roasting a hog, shimmering in its own fat on a rotating spit, a decorative apple in its mouth. The air wafted with the scent of roasted pork and charcoal.

The procession halted. Children in haloes and angels' wings fitted like rucksacks twirled to relieve their boredom. There was no time for delays; I wanted to get to the hospital before my grandmother fell asleep. I hoped it was nothing too serious. Perhaps it was a non-emergency procedure? Or flu that wouldn't go away? Oh, but what if she had cancer? Or Alzheimer's and couldn't remember who she was or who my mother was? Mosquitoes bit my leg. I swatted them with my palm and rubbed my knee. We were moving in slow motion.

Finally, we found an alleyway.

'Take the alley,' Lola Rosa instructed. 'It's a shortcut to the hospital.'

We floated up the silent side street lined with B&Bs. There was something sinister about the absence of noise on this well-lit street, punctuated only by the haunting echoes of Salve Regina and the slip-slap of disembodied feet in rubber slippers. I looked back to make sure Lola Rosa and Maya were behind me. They were swaddled in exhausted silence.

On reaching the end of the street, I burst into the empty space, running with a second wind that took me all the way to the white concrete building. Maya's footsteps behind me. We stopped at the entrance and waited for Lola Rosa to catch up.

Inside, the harsh lights and antiseptic white floors hurt my eyes. I approached the front desk. A woman with a neatly tied bun smiled before raising her index finger and passing a file to a colleague.

'Sorry about that, how can I help?' she asked.

'I'm looking for Alma Villar.'

She pulled out her filing cabinet drawer and retrieved a stack of folders, flipping through them until she reached letter V. She scanned it. 'I don't have an Alma Villar here. I'm sorry.'

'Can you please check again?'

She rolled her eyes, checked again. 'There's no one with that name here.'

My cheeks trembled. Either out of pity, or not wanting to appear cruel in front of the elderly couple behind me, she added: 'Your other option is Coron Town. That's the only other hospital she could be at. It's a big one.'

'Could we call them to check if she's there?' I asked. Surely there was a way to find out.

The receptionist next to her with a clove-shaped birthmark on her forehead explained the hospital couldn't give out patient information. 'Even if they could,' she said, 'their records aren't updated, so it isn't completely reliable. The surest way to check is to go there.'

What had I been expecting?

To find my grandmother. Just like that. For her to acknowledge me as her grandchild. Just like that. To love me. Just like that.

I pushed the double doors open, the humid air outside mingling with the musty air conditioning. The hairs on my arm stood on end. Maya and Lola Rosa stepped onto the pavement. They looked dishevelled, foreheads oily, wounds in places invisible to the eye.

Ahead of us, a young Reyna on a bubblegum-pink float gave the crowd a royal wave. She tilted forward and her floral crown swung precariously from the side of her head. She slid the wreath back in place. A column of men appeared behind her, dressed in brass band military jackets, the languid, liquid notes of Dios te Salve growing forceful. They were followed by a group of singing devotees holding candles. A woman ran after her naked toddler, his moon-bottom dusted white with talcum powder. I joined the swirling crowd. Trumpets, trombones, silk and chiffon, rosary prayers and despair all swept up in a surge of emotion. Maya and Lola Rosa trailed behind, sombre and unsmiling, as if they were part of a funeral procession.

WILL BINDLOSS

Will Bindloss writes stories about millennial anxieties in an age of encroaching technology and late-capitalist dread. He's working towards a collection and a debut novel. Pre-UEA, his career included stints as a copy editor and a gaming journalist. This is his first fiction publication.

willbindloss@gmail.com

Jolt
A short story

The power cuts and the PC lets out a kind of declining sigh, like an aeroplane's engine winding down. Mickey blinks at the blacked-out monitor. All that's left of its void-bound picture is the after-image on his retinas, which it goes without saying is a major downgrade. From 4k resolution to indeterminate fuzziness; from sixty frames per second to... what, one? It's like dream gaming, except way worse, because there's no prospect of waking up and doing some gaming for real. When it fades – and mmhmm, there it goes – there's nothing to do but stare into the dead screen. Not even a reflection in there.

Now Mickey's grimacing and shaking his head as the realisation lands. Another promotion series squandered. Another defeat grasped from the jaws of victory. He'll eat the leaver penalty while his matchmade teammates get the loss forgiven. Where's the justice in that? He puts those solo-queue mouth-breathers on his back all game, then courtesy of some National Grid balls-up, *he's* the one holding the bag. Yep, he'll cop the doubled-up ladder point hit. For something beyond his control! For something entirely not his fault!

You know what else is frustrating? That he's surrounded by devices that no longer function. He casts a pissed-off glance over their shadowy outlines: the compact form-factor mechanical keyboard, the high-def webcam, the gaming mouse on the gaming mousepad, the fuzzy-tipped USB mic, the surround-sound speakers, the panoramically curved ultra-wide monitor, the secondary screen, the tertiary screen. They mock him, somehow. In retaliation, he launches a kick into the intestinal tangle beneath his desk. Which – surprise – isn't satisfying at all, because the cables just give way and release a toe-coating cloud of dust.

It's not like cleaning hasn't occurred to Mickey. He knows what cleanliness looks like. He sees it all the time through the webcams of gaming streamers on Twitch.tv. Backdrops decked out with framed retro prints, curly neon signs, licensed plushies, subscriber-incentive pinboards; everything spotless, everything totally pristine. Back when Mickey streamed, he never bothered with that kind of windowdressing. Those careerists only did it to distract from their trash-tier gameplay. Not a problem for Mickey, so his viewers got his room as it was, as it still is. No green screen, just a taupe wall with a bald spot where the paint's peeling, against which viewers witnessed Mickey wig out over a variety of minor in-game setbacks. They tended not to stick around too long, the viewers. But no way was he going to censor his reactions to cater to the lowest common denominator. He raged because he *cared*. If they couldn't see that, screw them.

Anyway. Mickey regains some composure and grabs his phone from atop the computer tower. A swipe reveals the time: 11:47, which means the night's still young. And a WhatsApp notification: *Hiya. Just checking in. How goes uni? Know you're busy but maybe tomorrow evening give us a...* Enough preview to suss out what comes next. He bats it away on the lock screen to spare Mum the blue tick.

Now the six-inch display's bare save for the picture he's got set as a screensaver. It's from a year or so ago: him plus some buddies at MegaLAN in Sweden. His first and only in-person tournament. Nerds playing games on a strobe-lit stage, a crowd cheering them on – feels wild, even now. The high point of his 'pro' NexusQuest career. More accurately the buddies are teammates. In-game they were nicknamed LikeMeHarder, SugoiPanda, PlsNoCringe and GoodOKGreat. Mickey went by Michanix. He still does.

This was back when NexusQuest's esports scene was early-stage. Back when the metagame was breakable. Discover some new innovation and you could be looking at weeks of unchallenged dominance. In the picture, Mickey's riding one such glorious wave. He'd taken Gnarvil to the top lane. See, Gnarvil was designed as a mid-lane hero: that was always the basic Gnarvil paradigm. But Mickey saw untapped potential. He invented a maverick Gnarvil build with improved early-game itemisation and a radical new ability order. Opponents couldn't cope. Like, credit to his teammates, no shade, but their role was to facilitate Mickey's dominance. Even when enemies tunnel-visioned on shutting him down, he'd galaxy-brain his way out of it. Hero-select hard counter? Please, try harder. Three-on-one gank? Easy triple kill. It was non-stop big plays from Mickey. They smashed groups, then quarters, then semis. He barely even had to try.

Shame about the grand final. Yeah. Kind of a scandal how that went down. Still gives Mickey a sour taste. Probably that's why he didn't keep any physical mementoes. No branded merch, no ticket stubs. No framed version of that phone-screen pic. Lots of empty walls in here, come to think of it.

Still, what a grade A disgrace. They reach the final, then out of nowhere the devs drop an update nerfing Gnarvil into oblivion. Undid all his best item synergies, killed his cooldowns, kneecapped his ultimate. Those patch notes, ugh. *We've received a lot of feedback on how facing up against Gnarvil in the top lane can sometimes be an un-interactive experience. We're hoping these changes will level the playing field while still preserving this exciting new niche for everyone's favourite metamorphosing space-beetle.* Which was BS, because they knew full well the changes would massacre Gnarvil's competitive viability. And besides, Gnarvil's not a beetle, he's an armadillo.

Casuals on Reddit called the 3-0 loss a choke, but that was ridic, because what else could have happened? He had barely ten games of practice on his alt hero. Ditching Gnarvil was never in the plan because Gnarvil *was* the plan. Kind of stupid to think about. The five of them walking on stage, knowing their fate before they even sat in front of their keyboards.

The student house where Mickey lives has papier-mâché walls that somehow amplify every sound that passes through them. Right now his housemate Lucas is initiating a phone convo with his ad agency girlfriend.

'Hey. Hey. Hey, what's up? Guess what's—'

What sucks the most is how arbitrary it was. It's not like there was some dev-led conspiracy. In a parallel universe they drop that patch the next day. But the consequences. Jesus. The guys that trashed them got picked up by *ManaStorm,* an upstart esports org flush with venture capital dough. Luckboxed their way into salaries and sponsorships, scrimmages and practice schedules. While they were chilling in their LA-based gaming house, Mickey's team toughed it out once more in the online matchmaking crab barrel. Except not for long. Not after that league demotion set them on perma-tilt and forced them to disband for good.

Where are his old teammates now? Mickey doesn't know. Probably Stelios works for his dad's hotel business. Eric switched to poker. José trades stocks now. Rasmus learned coding. What remains is inactive Discord servers, abandoned theorycraft spreadsheets and friends list entries bearing the legend *Last online: a year ago.*

But, meh. Mickey's bored of flashing back. He thumbs the image away and flicks his phone's torch to On. He feels not great. Moments ago he was split-second reacting to brain-spiking stimuli; now he's tetchy and groggy with goosepimpled skin and fried synapses. Nothing new. It happens every time he logs out. He grinds his teeth in supermarket queues; he paces around the house waiting for takeout to arrive. He gets impatient at the kettle and the toaster. Reality's too low latency, that's the problem. Everything happens at a delay.

His back aches and his eyelids droop as he stares down the torch's lighthouse beam, which he's swivelled and fixed on the room's cheapy white door. A black cross of tape obscures the punch-dent he donated during his last red mist episode. He supposes he'll mosey down and see if a letter in the pile on the bottom-most stair can clarify the whole no-fucking-electric situation. He'll venture out into the street, scout out neighbouring windows, determine whether this thing's housewide or streetwide or whatever. Maybe he'll take out the rubbish while he's at it, since what else is there to do.

He peels himself off his *RaceBoy* gaming chair, reaches for the full-to-bursting bin bag squatting at the foot of his bed, hoists it up and he's in motion now, sucking in a lungful of air, wincing at the plastic's sharp rustle. He's through the door and down the stairs and in his head he hears the MegaLAN crowd, the roar that wasn't for him, the motorik of inflatable clappers beating close behind. From esports fame to solo-queue irrelevance. From amped-up in-the-moment flow to lowered stakes and washed-out boredom.

There's no letter downstairs, so he hits the pavement. A few neighbours linger outside open doors. Same deal everywhere, looks like. No street lights. No illumination in any of the houses either. The windows look like ability icons greyed out in a death screen.

Nothing doing, clearly. So the rubbish gets binned and Mickey turns around, pads back. Except as soon as he does there's a small cheer and a peripheral flickering and finally, yes! He's imagining the ding from dozens of resurrected appliances; the wind-tunnel whirr of his PC rebooting. Could there still be time to reconnect? A jolt runs through him as he grips the door handle, twists it, attempts to push... but like an idiot he's let it lock behind him. And – shit! – no keys in his pocket either. No choice but to hammer away and hope Lucas doesn't have headphones in.

He goes at it with both hands.

HANNAH COLE

Hannah Cole is the recipient of the 2020-21 Novelry Scholarship. Her work has been performed on student radio and longlisted for the Winter 2019 Reflex flash fiction competition. Her novel, *Win Her Back Wednesdays*, is a queer romantic comedy about reconnection and recovery via friendship.

hannah.s.cole@hotmail.co.uk

Win Her Back Wednesdays
An excerpt from a novel

There's a pub on the corner of her parents' street that exclusively serves seafood, and the only thing more certain than an upset stomach is the question that comes before the cheque: *so, are you seeing anyone?*

Jules has been a vegetarian for some time, so she orders solo chips and tries not to make eye contact with the lobster crawling around the tank to the left of their table. If this place wasn't owned by her father's best friend, she would think it was a front for some other enterprise. They're usually the only ones inside, even on a Saturday.

But it's Wednesday, and things are a little different: the special is smoked haddock, the jukebox is silent on account of the Women's Institute playing bingo two tables away, and Jules anticipates the question.

'Oh, did I tell you? I'm taking a break from...' Jules lifts her fingers to put the air quotes around her parents' spurious turn of phrase. 'Seeing anyone.'

Her father looks up from the dessert menu, even though he always orders the sticky toffee pudding with custard. Her mother nearly spits out her wine.

'You never mentioned it on the phone,' Susannah says. She calls every night to check Jules hasn't slipped in the shower or forgotten to turn off the stove. 'I thought you were finally thinking about dating again After Daniel.'

After Daniel is her family's version of *Anno Domini*. The year since Jules's break-up with Daniel has been, in their eyes, a new epoch of her life wherein the hopes and dreams they harboured for her are wilting, and she is a thing to be pitied and protected. They think Daniel was the best thing that has ever happened to Jules, and there will never be another like him.

The issue is, her family aren't wrong. She's spent the year pretending it doesn't hurt each time she gets out two mugs by default when making coffee, or notices his toothbrush still sitting in the bathroom cabinet. But if Jules admits this, they'll think she wants Daniel back or that she needs someone just like him. They will insist the panacea for loneliness is replacing what is lost with the next best thing.

She can't admit that she's going to be carrying her broken heart for a long time. She can't admit that it terrifies her, starting from the beginning, now she knows what it's like to have it all swept away.

So she has a plan.

'I *was* dating for a little while,' Jules says. 'Do you remember Casey?'

'That American lad you lived with at uni?' asks Russell.

'The very same.'

'You dated *him*?' Susannah demands.

'For about four months, yes.'

'And you didn't tell us?'

'It was a whirlwind romance, I suppose. We got caught up in the moment,' Jules tells them. 'The experience made me realise I'm not ready to get back out there.'

'But, sweetheart,' Susannah says, 'One bad egg doesn't ruin the omelette.'

'First of all, Mum, have you ever made an omelette in your life? And second, my experience with Casey has shown me there are some strange men in the world, and I'm not ready to expose myself to that.'

'Then date a few women,' Russell replies. 'Isn't that the point of being bisexual?'

'No, Dad, but thanks for trying.'

'I believe there's someone out there for everyone,' Russell tells her, and she almost wants to wrap those words around her soul like a warm blanket and believe in them unflinchingly. 'Don't give up so soon.'

'I'm not giving up. I'm taking a break.'

'How long will this break be?' Susannah asks.

'Longer than the transfer season, shorter than the One Direction hiatus,' Jules decides. 'Does that help?'

'Not at all.'

'I just need some time.'

She doesn't know how long it will take to get over Daniel. All she wants is to wake up one day and not think about him first. She doesn't believe that's the moment she should throw herself back into the business of longing and love. That is just the shape success has taken in her mind when she plots the trajectory of her healing.

'Oh, Juliet,' Susannah sighs, 'Don't you think you're running out of time?'

Jules glares at her mother, her attention tunnelling. She doesn't notice what is happening in the periphery of their conversation until they converge into a single disaster. The door swings open with a metallic chime, two members of the WI are descending into an argument about the height of their pampas grass, and Peter, the pub landlord, is approaching to pretend he doesn't know what they'll order for dessert. Jules cannot keep up until she hears a familiar voice call through time to her, like the first note of a forgotten favourite song.

'Hey, Jules,' Casey murmurs.

Casey is standing next to their table with his hands tucked into the pockets of a long woollen coat and his curls stuffed inside a baseball cap. It takes every ounce of Jules's self-preservation not to leap out of her chair and throw her arms around him. It's been so long, *too long*, and yet he's just like she remembers: easy smile, warm eyes, the kind of person whose hugs feel big and small at the same time, pushing aside the rest of the world while entirely filling its absence.

She doesn't know how it's possible to miss him more now that he's here, standing in front of her, but she is so filled with homesickness for him that she could cry.

'Speak of the devil,' Russell manages. 'I mean, good evening, Casey. How is life treating you?'

'This is Casey?' Susannah hisses, very loudly.

'Yes, this is Casey,' Jules confirms, exaggerating each word as she spins in her chair to face the man in question. 'What are you doing here?'

'I'm here to tell you I'm sorry,' Casey announces, glancing across to the WI's table. Their argument has fizzled out in favour of fresher fodder for their gossip mill. 'I should have told you about Josephine.'

'And Nathaniel,' Jules reminds him.

'And Nathaniel,' Casey agrees. There is a pause, and it's as if the whole pub is holding their breath, and then he adds: 'And Courtney.'

Jules is out of her chair in an instant. Peter skitters away, dropping the notepad he'd carried over under the pretence that they might surprise him with their order, and is quickly ushered into an empty chair at the WI's table.

'Courtney? You cheated on me with Courtney, too?'

'I thought you knew about Courtney,' Casey protests.

'Does it look like I knew about Courtney?'

'Well, I'm sorry I didn't tell you, but we were in the hot tub—'

'There was a *hot tub* at that party? How many other secrets are you keeping from me?'

'I would have told you, but you're allergic to chlorine.'

'I think I'd know if I was allergic to chlorine, Casey.'

'You are a little bit allergic to chlorine, sweetheart,' Susannah interrupts.

'See, you're a little bit allergic to chlorine.'

'Don't mansplain my allergies to me,' Jules snaps.

Casey rolls his eyes. 'Here we go again. I actually took a class about feminism in college and it's *not* mansplaining if—'

'Actually, it is mansplaining if, Casey,' Russell jumps in. 'Jules sent me this very useful infographic. I can forward it to you if you—'

'Dad!'

Russell shrinks back into his chair. 'Sorry.'

'I thought we agreed you would leave me alone,' Jules says, trying to steer them back onto the rehearsed course.

'I can't leave you alone,' Casey says. 'I think about you all the time.'

Jules crosses her arms firmly over her chest. 'We're over.'

'Back in my hometown, we have this tradition: win her back Wednesdays.' Casey tugs at her elbows until she relents and gives him her hands. 'Well, it's Wednesday, and I'm here to win you back.'

'Nothing you can say will—'

'Jules, you're the first girl I've been with for more than seventeen days. And my grandma's psychic told me I should marry a Scorpio with blue eyes, so you must be the one.'

Casey drops to one knee, and there's a collective gasp from her parents, Peter, and the entirety of the WI.

'Juliet Artemis Oatley, will you marry me?' Casey asks. 'Please say yes. Also, I'll need to borrow some money from your dad for the ring. And the wedding.'

Jules feels guilty, but not guilty enough *not* to do it, and the next thing she knows, she's slapping Casey clean across the face. He looks mildly shocked for a moment before clattering to the floor. His hat falls off and skids beneath Peter's chair. He gets dust all over the elbows of his fancy coat, which he swipes off with an exaggerated flick of his wrists as he sits up.

'You might be giving up on – thank you.' Casey gets momentarily sidetracked by a lady from the WI helping him back to his feet. 'You might be giving up on us, Jules, but I *never* will.'

'I think you should go,' Jules tells him.

'Fine. But we'll never be over, Jules,' Casey pledges solemnly.

'We already are.'

There's a stretch of silence, broken when Peter reaches underneath his chair and procures Casey's baseball cap. He hands the hat over, and Casey ruffles his hair before pulling the cap back on.

'Goodbye, Casey,' Jules says pointedly.

'I'll see you around,' Casey says to Jules. He puts his hands back into his pockets and strolls out of the pub like he's just won a friendly game of pool with the locals and has been called home for dinner.

Jules collapses back into her chair and covers her face with her hands. 'I'm *so sorry*, Peter. If I had any idea Casey would do something – well, something so romantic...'

Susannah and Russell exchange a horrified look.

'I had no idea he cared,' Jules presses on. She throws a longing look at the door. 'Maybe I should go after him—'

'No! Juliet Oatley, under no circumstances are you going after that boy,' Susannah snaps.

'But—'

'I think it's best you let him go,' Russell adds more gently.

Jules sighs, putting all of her tormented adolescent lovesickness into the sound. 'I think I love him.'

Her mother glances in askance at her father again and, in that moment, Jules knows she has won.

The moment Jules gets back to her flat, Susannah calls.

'Hi, Mum,' Jules answers, holding the phone to her ear with her shoulder.

'Did you get home safely?' Susannah asks.

'Evidently.'

'Juliet.'

'Yes, Mum, I got home safely.'

'Good. Good.' There's a beat of silence. 'Sweetheart, I was thinking about what you said about taking a break from dating.'

'Oh?'

'And I agree. Maybe you do need time to understand what you want from a relationship, and to find someone who... shares your goals.'

'If you think so.'

'I do think so,' Susannah replies. 'It was lovely seeing you tonight, despite...'

'I'm sorry about Casey.'

'Oh, that's all right. It was interesting.'

Jules tries not to laugh. 'That's one word for it.'

'We're going to bed now, but you can call in the night if you need anything.'

Jules can't help smiling, even though her mother tells her this every night. Even though Susannah will almost certainly leave her phone downstairs to charge and not hear any emergency calls. 'Thank you.'

'Love you.'

'Love you, too. Speak to you soon.'

'Buh-bye!'

Jules ends the call, but she doesn't lock the phone. Instead, she opens and types an email, the newest in a long chain:

To: Casey Hallahan
From: Juliet Oatley
Subject: RE: Win Her Back Wednesdays

are you still on for lunch tomorrow? it would be nice to see you. again. properly.

CONOR DUGGAN

Conor Duggan is an Irish writer of short stories, limerick poems, and prose. Before studying fiction in Norwich, he studied and worked as a geologist. He is a fan of comedy, word play, and puns.

dugganch@tcd.ie

The Egg and the Skipping Rope
A short story

I opened my first art gallery when I was seven years old. Mr Holloway told me the best artists named their galleries after the street they lived on, so I named mine *Galerie Rue Saint-Jacques*. It opened once a week, on Saturday mornings, when I knew my best patron, Matthew Holloway, would be passing by on his way back from the village, carrying fresh baguettes that looked like biros in his enormous hands.

He was the tallest man I knew and his head was the only one that I ever saw reach above the front hedge. His steps were so big that his head would come in and out of view, as though someone was bouncing a large rubber egg off the footpath on the other side. When I saw the egg bouncing towards the village, I'd message in on a pretend radio made from my hand and say, 'Shh, the egg is in the village. Repeat. The egg is in the village.' Then I'd hurry inside and get my art ready for display.

Northern France always seemed to have good weather, especially on Saturdays, so I'd set my paintings on the patio behind our red-brick house. There was a piece cracked off the patio, with a small cavity behind it, and one day I pulled it away and there was a huge rat inside. I stood there, frozen. I didn't know what to do, so I just put the piece of concrete back in its place. My mam said it was a possum when I described it to her because it had a long thin snout, but I told everyone it was a rat anyway.

When her friends came over, I'd say, 'Be careful where you sit. There's a rat in the garden.'

'That wasn't a rat,' my mother would say back, 'it was a possum.'

'It was a rat. A big fat one too.'

—

One of my paintings on display was of a great big shining sun, that was so big I had to draw it as an oval so that it would fit on the page. It was inspired by a stand-off I'd had with my teacher, Monsieur Desén. We fell out over the weather.

Every day in school, someone different was picked to draw the weather on a special chart in the corner of the classroom. Whoever was picked was given the website www.meteofrance.fr and instructions on a piece of paper for how to look it up.

The row happened on a nice day. The sky was blue, with just a few specks of cloud, and it was warm enough that some teachers were even teaching their classes outside. I was picked, and I drew a sun so huge it had to be drawn as an oval to fit on the whiteboard.

'*T'as pas oublié quelque chose?*'

Did you forget something?

'*Non.*'

'*T'es sûr?*'

'*Oui.*'

Monsieur Desén pushed down on his hairy arms, lifting himself from behind his desk, and erased the sun from the weather chart. He explained that we had some cloud today and asked if I could redraw the picture.

I drew a full sun again.

He looked straight at me and wiped the board clear for the second time. He said I had to draw the clouds because it was a cloudy day.

I was getting cross. I made these big, puffy breaths as though I was trying to inflate myself up to his size. '*D'accord,*' I said. But instead of picking up the whiteboard marker, I picked up the permanent marker we used to name our art folders and I drew the big oval sun again, with rays of sunlight coming off it in all directions.

'It's a perfect day and you don't even know it!' I screamed at him.

I started crying and the school rang home. Mam could speak French and she went to the school to hear the good news. Dad couldn't and he went to the school to ignore the bad; Monsieur Desén tersely handed me over to him.

This was my first painting for viewing, and it was called, *Monsieur Desén's Favourite Weather*.

—

'Shh, the egg is coming back, the egg is coming.' I would get my position ready and stand by my paintings with my arms folded behind my back. The lock on the wooden gate in the hedgerow would clink open and in would come Matthew Holloway.

'*Bonjour Monsieur.*' I'd bow.

My mam would come out then and they'd say hi and do cheek-kisses even though neither of them were French. Then she'd take his bread inside and prepare fresh coffee while he'd examine my paintings.

He'd muse aloud while he leaned down to inspect them.

'Hmm... sunny,' he said, while looking at *Monsieur Desén's Favourite Weather*, 'Lucy did say she was looking for ways to brighten up the kitchen.' I'd listen to every word and look for clues as to which one he'd buy.

He went to the next painting, of a bag of flour with roses sticking out of it. 'I do love to bake, but I'm not sure how pleased Lucy would be to find thorns in her sponge cake... I better go discuss the options with your father.' And with that, he'd head down the patio to the decking chairs and sit and chat with my father, the coffee ready, and the patisserie he brought with him plated and cut into slivers on the table.

Then would come The Great Wait. After hassling Mam in the kitchen, I'd go upstairs to my parents' room and open the window slightly. Then I'd lie down on the beige carpet and listen to my father and Matthew talking down below. I learnt lots of stuff through that window. I knew about Tony Blair and Jacques Chirac. I didn't know who the IRA were, but I learnt the word 'ceasefire'. Shania Twain, tumours, Oasis, boob jobs.

My ears pricked when I heard my dad tell him about the phone call from Monsieur Desén, which my sister had to translate, and the two of them, thinking that no one was listening, let out big laughs.

Matthew said, 'I am surprised he didn't scrub it off with that big moustache of his.'

I was rolling around laughing at that one.

I could tell when he was about to leave because there would be a slight pause in the conversation, and then Matthew would say, 'I better get back to Lucy.'

Lucy was the only woman I knew who had pigtails. She was tall too, not tall enough for her head to be seen over the hedge, but tall enough that her pigtails would bounce up and down into view. When the two of them walked by the house together, they became The Egg and The Skipping Rope.

Matthew bought *Monsieur Desén's Favourite Weather* for ten francs that day, then the lock on the gate clinked and the egg bounced home.

—

Mam started going to the Holloways' house to help Lucy. Lucy never needed help before, so I asked my mam what she was doing over there. 'Making sandwiches,' she said. One of the days I went with her to the Holloways' because there was no one at home to mind me. We stopped in *Shopi* to buy bread.

I guarded the trolley while she went into the vegetable aisle for salads. I didn't want to see cauliflowers. Mam had sat with me on the stairs to explain, 'It can come in two ways. Some are shaped like a golf ball and some like a cauliflower. Matthew's is like a cauliflower, so they can remove the big bit but they're not able to remove all the small bits. And the small bits can grow back.'

After lunch, Lucy and my mam went into the garden to sunbathe because it was a nice day. Lucy had poured me a glass of apple juice with a straw in it and asked if I'd bring it in for Matthew. The Holloways' hallway was big and open with white tiles and the TV room was in an alcove just off it. I stopped around the corner from the alcove and stood against the wall. I could hear French cartoons and there was a breeze.

When I went in, Matthew was sitting on the couch. He was all puffy like the Michelin Man. He didn't look fat but as if someone had used a pump and pumped him up. His skin was shiny and a fan was blowing air at him. His eyes moved and he saw me, but his head stayed still.

I went to put the juice down and the TV remote fell off the coffee table. The cartoon switched over to nine mini-screens with blue channel listings down the side. Matthew started making groaning noises.

They had gotten a big satellite dish and they had 399 channels. There were two remotes and they sometimes needed to be used together. I tried to change it back and the channel changed to a blur of black and white and made a fuzzing noise. Matthew started making loud 'ughhhh' sounds. I didn't know what to do, so I ran away, and Matthew was left, stuck there looking at a wall of black and white.

Lucy found me in the utility room. 'He's turning into the Michelin Man,' I cried.

Dad started reading the Sunday paper at the Holloways' and, unlike Mam and the sandwiches, I knew what he was doing. When he came home, I would lie on the floor in the front room with my eyes closed and Dad would describe what was going on up there.

'So, I had a coffee in the alcove and Matthew had his apple juice... I read him out the news that Tony Blair got in – he enjoyed that one... then he starting having a snooze, so I turned on *Street Sharks* before I left, because I know he'll like that on when he wakes up.'

He took a small parcel out of his pocket and handed it down to me.

'I was also given this,' he said.

I opened the brown parcel. Inside was a paintbrush and a note written in big difficult writing:

'Where is *le petit artiste*?'

'Looks like you're being commissioned,' said Dad with a wink.

—

I had a painting I'd been preparing in secret for Matthew for the next time he came to visit *Galerie Rue Saint-Jacques*. Mam wanted to check it before we brought it over, to make sure it was suitable, but I said if anyone looked at it before Matthew, I'd scream. I kept it wrapped in a beach towel on my lap in the car.

When we got there, Lucy had the alcove ready and Matthew looked like he was on holiday because he was wearing a Hawaiian shirt and there was an umbrella in his apple juice.

I set the painting up on the coffee table and pulled the towel off. Lucy and Mam both said that it was lovely straight away, but I knew they didn't know what it was. 'Is it *Monsieur Desén's Favourite... Sunset*?'

The bottom half of the page was all green. Above the green poked a big egg. And going over the top of the egg was a yellow rope.

Matthew made a noise and when Lucy leaned in to hear him, he lifted his finger and flicked one of her pigtails. I started laughing and Matthew made more noises which I knew was him laughing too. Lucy and Mam started laughing as well, although I knew they still didn't get it. It was only me and Matthew who knew what was going on. Only Matthew found my art funny and that's why he will always be my greatest patron.

ISABEL EDAIN

Isabel Edain was born in smoky Sheffield and graduated from UEA last year. They are interested (in no particular order) in Decadent literature, folklore, dead Russians, queer love, and ghosts. It would be nice to be a poet, but they are definitely a novelist.

sucrimgible@gmail.com

Moth & Meredith
The opening of a novel

Meredith, amongst other things, was gifted with an excellent sense of doom. She felt it like other people felt shadows sliding over a patch of sun, or somebody watching them. She had once tried to articulate this to a beautiful girl at a party who giggled and said, 'How morbid,' and this worried her, for she did not particularly want to be morbid yet she seemed to be stuck with it.

Death itself did not seem to her a morbid thing. *Morbid* was a human word, more human than most words: it meant that death was strange and bad, so being interested in death was also strange and bad. And Meredith was interested in death, but she was also interested in not being bad. She felt that it was desperately important not to be bad. There was a reason she felt this way, or perhaps it was not a reason so much as a small luminous thing that lived at the back of her brain, a hard core of light that said *be good*.

But surely it was possible to be good and also to be interested in Pictish burial rites, and embalming, and what flowers people chose for funerals. Conor, her boyfriend, refused to enter her room ever since he found upon her desk a dead and lavishly gorgeous blue tit, the painterly sheen of whose feathers seemed to hold a terrible mystery. He had yelped and reeled back.

Conor did not like death.

Meredith did not really understand this. Death was something one found in hedgerows and cemeteries and the black spots on people's fingernails: it was quite ordinary.

Doom was something else. Doom crept after people.

Meredith always knew when it was there. She had met it first in the black pit of her mother's living room, and again much later in the shape of a man. Yet when she tried to explain it to Conor, he put a pillow over his head and said, 'La la la la, I can't hear you, you're being morbid, I can't hear you.' That was Conor.

Conor was extravagant. Sometimes he was childish and drank too much beer and started shouting at strangers and calling them names. Sometimes he would go into sulks for days and days, and Meredith would wait patiently for him to return her calls.

But he also liked to braid her hair in fanciful ways, and run her absurdly scented bubble baths, and bring her strange trinkets from wherever he went: a necklace with a silver fox charm, a battered Anne Rice novel, a plastic friendship bracelet from a vending machine, fern-embroidered tights, a chocolate bar. He was gifted with a vast vocabulary and a pale luminous face over which an occasional gold curl tenderly blew.

Meredith reminded herself of these things; she reminded herself often, for Conor was quite an incorrigible flake. Conor missed everything. Buses, lectures, dates where Meredith had been left standing outside art galleries in the snow, shoe fittings, breakfast, appointments – so many appointments, with the doctor and the jobcentre and his academic advisor. Sometimes Meredith wondered if she had any power to hold him at all.

There was only one thing that Conor didn't miss – that he never missed – and that was supper at his father's house on Sunday night.

Each Tuesday, Meredith came downstairs to find a snowy, pristine card on her doormat that pronounced, in scrolling black ink:
Dear Miss Meredith Quinton
We would be delighted to invite you to supper this Sunday at 7 p.m.,
   Clerkin Street, The Holding.
Please let us know if you can make it.
Best wishes,
Lucian and Anna Duke

Meredith loved these snowy cards, which Conor received too, and saved them because throwing away something so visibly luxurious felt like a travesty. And every week, or almost, she put on one of her favourite dresses and met Conor at the end of her road, and together they walked to the tall stone house on Clerkin Street that Lucian Duke had bought and named the Holding.

Lucian Duke was a Professor of Philosophy at the University of Nottingham, where Meredith studied Archaeology and Conor studied History of Art. Lucian lived in the Holding with Conor's stepmother Anna. Anna was kind and immensely stylish; she owned books about gin tasting and cocktail dresses embroidered in gold. She bought Conor shirts in violet and green and joked to Meredith about male folly. And Meredith loved her, but she loved Lucian Duke more, for he was everything she thought a professor should be, like a character from a book.

Lucian Duke had eyes that were both sad and merry and a head of silver curls less pristine than his shirts. He told jokes, which were sometimes quite good, over red wine at dinner and talked gravely to Meredith about transmigration of the soul over whisky in the library afterwards. There were waiting lists for his classes and queues for his lectures, and in the Holding he had made a place of enormous grace. The Dukes seemed to own nothing that did not fit Lucian's peculiar philosophy of beauty. He adored the lavish and useless detail: the violet filigree of a peacock feather, the hopeless purity of crystal bells. When Lucian stood like a god in its cavernous hallway, the Holding seemed to have moulded itself around him, to have taken on the shape or shadow of his soul.

It was a Georgian house, pale grey and gently crumbly, poetic with honeysuckle. A house of silver candelabras and a belching Aga and a vast kitchen table, a single, polished, pockmarked slab. And oddities. Lucian was no minimalist. Russian dolls, sculptures of birds, a taxidermied albino rat...

And books. Books piled upon the stairs, shelved above the toilet, lining the walls on the landing. The first time she walked in and saw them, Meredith had known that she could trust Lucian and Anna. Sometimes, deep inside herself, she wondered if she trusted Lucian and Anna more than she trusted Conor. There was something that tugged, whenever she looked at Conor, at her innards; she was not sure whether it was love or her sense that he was doomed.

It was past eight o'clock. In the kitchen, the Aga hissed gently.

They had finished dinner. The table was a pile of ugly scraps: a dish of greasy black rags (tahini-roasted aubergines), a brown carcass (chicken stuffed with sultanas and almonds), cracked and derelict shells (quail's eggs).

The food was always good at the Holding.

Meredith felt nice: she felt flushed and happy and frightfully clever. She had a vague idea, at the back of her head, that this was because Lucian and Anna were good at making people feel this way. But she was wearing her favourite dress of dim dark velvet, and she had been living in her pyjamas for weeks, but she was out of them now, and she had drawn tiny silver stars above her eyes. She was sipping white wine and although she didn't know much about wine, she thought it was very nice. One part of her was thinking this and another part was dreaming, listening to the dark wind rattle the windowpanes.

Conor was a long, messy presence beside her. Conor, like a jack-in-the-box, always seemed to sprawl slightly out of the space he occupied. Conor, in a green silk shirt, pink-cheeked with wine, his hair curling madly at the ends, was telling a meandering story about the time he found a shopping trolley in the river. 'And then he just let it go, did old Sam. Just let it plop back into the river to rust away there for a thousand verdigris years.'

Anna and Lucian were laughing somewhat indulgently.

'So I gather you're both studying hard?' said Anna, one eyebrow raised.

Conor stabbed at a shred of chicken. 'Merry's been studying herself blind, you know her. I wish I had a speck of her morale.'

Lucian tipped the wine bottle up to refill Meredith's glass. 'How are *you* finding things, Meredith?'

She laid down her fork – carefully, for it was silver, slim as a lily. 'Oh, I'm OK,' she said and hesitated. With her mother she would have stopped there. Not because her mother didn't want to hear Meredith's problems, quite the opposite, her mother would be horrified. Then she would tell Meredith to stop doing anything that even mildly inconvenienced her, to dab lavender oil on her temples, to make a protection pouch and, also, probably, to drop out of university.

But Anna and Lucian were looking at her with the mild yet infinitely friendly curiosity of academic deities. Meredith hazarded, 'Actually, I'm a bit stressed. My field write-up's due in a week and I'm supposed to be picking my dissertation project soon. But the labs are flooded and—'

'She's fine,' Conor whispered.

Lucian, ignoring him, said, 'And how are your dreams?'

She frowned. 'Well... they've been a bit strange. Lots of corridors that all look the same. The Shark keeps appearing. Gliding through the walls...'

Conor downed his glass of wine.

Lucian nodded. 'Ah, the Shark. Is that bad?'

'I don't know. I'm never sure. It seems like it's scared of something.' She paused, gauging whether he was still listening; as always, he was, carefully. 'And the Stag With No Antlers is restless. He keeps stomping his silver feet and scraping up sparks.'

'His hooves,' said Conor. He had begun to fidget. He was tearing a shred of paper into smaller and smaller pieces so that it flaked down like dandruff.

'Sorry?' said Meredith.

'His hooves.' There was a pause. 'Stags have hooves.'

'But he's not a stag, remember?' said Meredith. 'He doesn't have any antlers.'

Conor let the last shreds of paper fall to the tablecloth. 'Can we just stop talking about it?' he said.

Lucian leaned closer. 'You know, Meredith, De Quincey thought that dreams were places of terrible power. He wrote of them as the "one great tube through which we communicate with the shadowy." I think he would have been very interested in yours.'

Meredith sensed Conor's discomfort and felt guilty but replied. 'I don't know. I don't know if I'm communicating with anything much. All of them – the Shark, the Mermaid, the Albatross, the Stag – they're sort of just like people you pass on the street to me, you know? I—'

'Can we just change the subject?' said Conor.

Lucian turned to his son. 'What's the matter, Conor?'

Conor fiddled with his fork. 'Nothing,' he said. 'It's boring.'

Lucian opened his mouth, but at that moment, Anna stood up and said, brightly, 'I don't suppose anyone wants dessert?'

'God, yes,' said Conor.

Lucian looked down at the table. 'A question never quite worth the asking, one feels.'

'Not with these two,' said Anna. 'You should meet the rest of the professors. Dinners are a nightmare. Everybody has something wrong with them that means they can't eat something or other. It's a symptom of too much academia if you ask me.'

'I'm allergic to strawberries,' Lucian reported to Meredith.

Anna made a shocked face and tutted expansively, then she kissed Lucian. Conor wrinkled up his nose in horror.

Meredith looked away, but she felt rather fascinated by Lucian and Anna's marriage. She could not imagine a world in which her mother had someone other than Meredith herself. Sometimes it was hard to believe that her father was a real man with a physical existence and that she had not simply been found upon a bed of phantom roses or carried to her mother's arms in the wings of a great grey bird.

But after all, Conor did not know his own mother either. Or that was what he said.

The kiss was over.

'Everyone's a hypochondriac,' said Lucian cheerfully.

'I think academic life could make anyone a hypochondriac,' said Meredith.

Conor huffed to signal that he was bored with the conversation.

POLLY HALLADAY

Polly Halladay is a Norwich/London-based writer with a BA in English Language and Literature. She writes magical realist fiction with a focus on the strangeness and horror of womanhood and is currently working on a collection of short stories. Other works in development include a bildungsroman novel about ghosts and grooming.

polly.g.halladay@gmail.com

She Visits
An extract from a short story

You were either a believer or you weren't, at first. Psychiatric hospitals filled; the emergency services were overwhelmed. Cults formed and were broken. Schools closed and opened. Then there were national polls and social media surveys trying to keep track of those who could see them. 'Seers' we were termed, though that suggests a degree of wisdom which is misplaced.

There were interviews attempted, but they didn't show up on the screen, adrift between the pixels. You couldn't hear them either, their voices lost amid frequencies. Thirty-three million people tuned in to the *News at Six* to watch an empty chair, the interviewer questioning silence.

Eventually, we just got on with it, accepted the new normal. At the café, it was business as usual.

It was mid-morning, and I was smoking in the summer heat, leaning by the bins on the backstreet, when I saw one sitting beside the junkie outside the kebab shop.

Something sordid about seeing the backs of establishments: wheelie bins released from their steel-shutter cages, mouths agape, spewing split black liners on the ground, used tissues, rotten food, and the staff's stolen cigarette breaks butted into the hot pavement.

The junkie looked happier than usual, more animated than I'd ever seen him, more alive. He was chatting with it, both of them reclined on a cardboard box. Then the junkie passed the needle – unusually generous of him, I thought – and it took it. Holding something solid, it looked even more incorporeal than before, blending with the heatwaves rippling in the distance. I had to keep blinking to hold it in sight.

It must have slipped the needle into the nothing of its arm because after a moment, it disappeared. The needle fell to the ground, a sound of splintered glass. But the junkie was too busy slapping his wrist, opening and closing his fist, to notice.

I stubbed out my cigarette, tipped the dregs of my coffee away, and walked back inside the café to work.

—

Meanwhile, a mother. Tries to pour her son some cereal. But she can't lift the box. Can't smell the milk to see if it's off. Can't speak. Or kiss him goodbye as he leaves. His father lies grief-soiled on the sofa, didn't teach the boy to tie his own shoelaces or take himself to school. She cries. Silent in the kitchen. Her tears don't even fall.

—

I took my lunch out the back: more cigarettes and caffeine, no stomach for anything else. The junkie was gone, the midday sun too much for skin and bone. Simon heard me coming back inside and called for me from the office, a pustule of space squeezed into the head of the café. Above it, your average overpriced London flat was perched like an expensive hat. Either side, 'chic' eateries, boutiques, and international restaurants constituted the high street of this urban village on the outskirts of the city.

I tied my milk-stained and stinking apron around me quickly, as I climbed the narrow stairway made of cheap, unpainted plywood – only staff were allowed back there. Places like this: faux industrial décor, shining metal tabletops, gleaming marble counters, all smoke and mirrors really. Food hygiene offences in the kitchen, mop water black and Guinness-thick, and stained steel tables polished with baby oil to complete the illusion. A veneer of sophistication veiling filth. A plaster on a pock-marked arm. The polish I used to cover my coffee-stained nails.

I stood just inside the office, silent at the top step, anticipating a grilling. I'd opened late, broken three cups over the course of the morning, and just finished my fourth cigarette break in as many hours. Simon, the manager, was sitting on a shitty little chair, his laptop humming on a shitty little desk. The rest of the office, and there wasn't much of it, was taken up with large black shelves half-full of stock. Disposable cups, tumescent tubs of mayonnaise, an industrial-sized bag of chocolate buttons – Anita, the other barista, would sneak me one, cupped in her hand like treasure, and pop it, already softened by the heat of her skin, into my mouth – and a freezer you could hide a body in.

Simon tapped away for a full minute, knee jerking, while I stood there. Then he sighed, rubbed his stubbled jaw, and swivelled on the chair to look at me. It was hard to place his age: greying at the temples, thinning on top, the skin beneath shiny like linoleum. But something young about how he moved, flitting from task to task, always doing, never satisfied with any job done.

'Do you like this job?' he asked.

No. 'Yes,' I said.

'Do you want to progress in this job?'

No. 'Yes,' I said.

'Are you trying to get yourself fired?'

No. 'No,' I said. It was true. The café was all I'd known for the past half-decade. It was simple, insignificant. It passed the time. It paid the bills.

'What the fuck is going on with you then?'

I thought about them. The news reports trickling in over the radio downstairs. The sirens multiplying in the night. But mainly, I thought about her.

It was the evening before, still light but waning. I was looking in my bathroom mirror. I wasn't admiring my reflection; there was nothing admirable in my face. I was wiping off the make-up smudged into my skin during the hot shift, using the good stuff that stings because you shouldn't use it on your eyes, but it's the only thing that works. I opened my eyes, and I saw her.

She wasn't there, and then she was. Grey, as they all are, but a boring kind of grey. The shade you see without seeing it, that resides within every other colour, that rims every shadow, when white is never truly white, not really. That's the grey, the colour without colour.

She wasn't a shimmering sign of life after life, like you might want her to be, or glistening ethereally. She wasn't the grisly kind; no blood, swollen veins, or rotting flesh peeling from her cheeks. No old sheet thrown over either, the bulge of a head beneath and two black slits for eyes. Just grey. Mute grey. But not mute. She cried 'Boo!' of course, just because she could. And I jumped, of course, because she made me fucking jump.

She probably thought my red, watering eyes were the result of her trickery. She laughed hollowly and floated through my bathroom door. Mainly, I was just pissed off – it had been a long shift.

Simon had gone on about the state of the café floor, stood there sniffing, watching me while I mopped it. I'd closed the doors; Simon didn't waste money on aircon and without the slight breeze off the busy street, the sweat ran down in rivulets. He must have noticed my melting face, the shadow coming loose around my eyes. I'd been embarrassed, though I didn't find him remotely attractive. Frustrated, I'd snatched the scourer to scrub the corners where the counter met the floor, black from years of congealed coffee grounds. Crouched like an animal, I'd scrubbed hard, grunting, wanting him to see how ugly I could be. We'd closed at six but didn't get out until eight and Simon didn't pay overtime.

I decided not to be a coward and opened the bathroom door, following her like a stalker might as she glided into the main room of my garret flat: kitchen, living, and dining, shoved together like unwilling siblings in a family photograph. Standing just inside the room, as though a stranger in my own home, I watched her roam about.

Her presence fluctuated, nearly erased in the low light of the evening sun through the window. More substantial in the shadows: by the bookshelf, behind the door, in the corner where the roof slanted into the room. She went to the fridge and with a touch of annoyance, her fingers slipping through the handle, she opened it. Looking inside, she snorted, then moved over to the sofa, fingering the frayed blanket I'd thrown over it to cover the stains from the previous tenant. Then she regarded the only picture I'd bothered to frame: a photo, the friends and family pictured mere spectres beneath a film of thick dust. Unimpressed, she pushed the corner down with her finger, repositioning the frame on a wonk, some dust falling and speckling the sofa. At the bookshelf, she noted my small collection: novels from forgotten days, unanswered letters from lost friends, folders with old documents inside. With comparative ease, she drew a folder out, opened it and flicked through the plastic wallets. Settling on one, she pulled out my degree certificate and, turning to look right at me, dropped it to the floor.

'Right,' I said, crossing my arms, looking anywhere but her face. 'Who the fuck are you and what are you doing in my flat?' She just smiled.

She hung around all evening, flickering in the middle of the room, making small, judgemental noises when I drank for dinner.

'I'll get the exorcist round,' I told her, if she kept that up. Trying to joke, to sound OK, but perched on the arm of the sofa, close to the window, which I tried not to regard as a potential escape route.

Hours passed, and all she seemed to do was grow more restless: tucking in chairs, reordering the shoe rack, testing the dry beds of my potted plants. I wondered if she could feel anything with those fingers, long and slender like mine, but tapering at the ends into nothingness.

Empty bottles sprouted around me, but the alcohol didn't work like it usually did, my nerves keeping me alert, and as the sun relinquished its hold, if not its heat, on the night, I noticed something. The tips of her fingers seemed to solidify, her edges becoming more discernible, more familiar. I looked away, as though seeing something I shouldn't have, as though by seeing, I was not only acknowledging her presence but strengthening it. I skirted her on my way to bed.

When I woke, the bottles were gone. She was in the cupboard, a carton of out-of-date eggs in one hand and a bag of stale cereal in the other. I shut the door quickly and left without breakfast. It was only when I'd reached the café that I realised I'd forgotten the key, not in its usual place in my bag.

I lived right around the corner but trudged back, the sun sharp and unforgiving. She was there – I hadn't really expected her to leave – and the key was in the middle of the table, glowing in the bright morning light. She was out of the cupboard, barely visible in the sun shining through her from the window. I was thankful for that. It helped me sound assertive when I said, 'Next time, tell me when I forget to take the keys, yeah?'

She didn't respond, and I realised on the walk back to the café that, in saying that, I'd inadvertently invited her to stay.

—

Meanwhile, an old man. Wakes under an old quilt in an old bed that creaks as he rises. The old man also creaks, his joints like joints get.

The old woman doesn't wake beside him. Doesn't rise as he does. Doesn't creak. She is silent, sitting in the old armchair opposite the bed, nude, not yet dressed for the day. Folds of her grey skin hang through the wicker arms and the wicker back of the chair. She bends, pulls grey stockings suddenly at her ankles up her legs, covering the grey varicose veins entwining her grey calves. Then she rises without creaking, the wicker chair unwincing, and walks to the wardrobe. Opening its doors and reaching inside, she pulls grey dresses from their coloured selves like banana skins. She puts one on. Then she leaves her dead self in the bed.

MYRIAL A HOLBROOK

Myrial A Holbrook is from Columbus, Ohio. Before coming to UEA, she earned a bachelor's in Comparative Literature from Princeton University and an MPhil in Education from the University of Cambridge. Her creative writing is published in *Flip the Page, The Nassau Literary Review,* and *Coffin Bell.* She is writing her first novel.

myrialholbrook27@gmail.com

The Land Is Darkened

The following is an excerpt from a historical novel set in Eastern Kentucky and spanning one family's history, from the Shawnee presence and white settlement in the 1790s through to the late nineteenth century. This section takes place a few years after the end of the American Civil War.

It is a late night in late winter. The silence of the snow makes a world unto itself. Somewhere deep in their burrows, the groundhogs sleep and grow thin as beanstalks. In the old days, when it was cold and dark, and there was nothing better to do than stretch achy limbs and untangle old yarns before the fire, the Judge would be sharing drinks with Horatio. 'Bevvies,' the Judge called them. 'Blazers,' Horatio called them.

The Judge sits by the fire under a scratchy horse blanket, sipping a mix of whiskey and cider. The whiskey was aged in his father's white oak barrels and dates from before the war. The cider is from last fall's paltry harvest, and tastes it. Despite forty years of nurturing attentions over three generations, the orchard, after a few years' neglect, has turned irredeemably sour. The Judge smacks his tongue at the acid but feels a strange, punitive satisfaction as it flames down his throat and into his belly.

The drink, best hot, is tepid now. He is too indifferent to warm it again. If there were company, perhaps. But there is none, and there will be none. Not the Reverend Gresham, who went back east during the war, not the hawker with his clinking tin wares and cross-eyed mule, not even that blasted upstart surveyor Diggins who used to lope the peripheries like a starved wolf, angling for a dispute. Nowadays, there are neither properties nor property owners in abundance to rustle up fuss enough for a dispute.

'Nothing to look forward to, nothing at all,' the Judge mumbles to himself, swirling his drink, listening to the whistles of the outside winds, feeling their drafty offspring slither through the invisible gaps in the chinking.

The Judge hears the cow lowing in the stable and sets down his drink on the mantel, draping the blanket around his shoulders and picking up the tin pail by the door. Poor girl, she'd taken the loss of her calf hard this year, though God knows he needed the veal and milk to get through the winter. And since the old mare died, she had no one for company except the Judge. He opens the door and starts down the slippery path to the stable.

In the moonlight, beyond the pastures and the skeletal orchard, his adjusting eyes sketch the outline of a distant, creeping shadow. Even at such a distance in the blackness, he can see that it is a horse, all skin and bones. The rider holds a bundle before him. A red scarf tied around the rider's head waves like the herald flag of a royal procession.

For a moment the Judge recalls with a jolt of child's terror Katee-nan's wandering spirits, who, she used to say, prowl about on lonely nights like these, seeking sanctuary that can't be found.

'They're wanderers,' she explained to him and his brother Beady as boys. 'Like we Shawnee are wanderers. But where we have death, they have nothing. Not life, not death, but somewhere in between. They are a skin without a skeleton, a spirit without past or future.'

As the figure creeps closer, the Judge shivers in the cutting cold and feels the numbness overcome his fingers and the tip of his nose. He sees the horse stumble on the path, favoring its right side. Its light gray coat glistens with sweat in the moonlight.

'Ho there!' the Judge calls out, his breath a billow. The figure straightens up, clutching the bundle closer and pulling the reins.

'Hullo, Judge!'

The Judge drops the pail in chuckling excitement and lights over at a jog.

'Horatio, you rascal, whyn't you write a fella once in a while? You don't know how plum glad I am to see you now, in the lively flesh.'

'It's mutuary, Judge. Lookee who I've brung with me.'

He uncovers the bundle, revealing the upturned face of a little girl. She looks at Horatio sleepily, then peers down at the Judge.

'Could this be your grandbaby?' the Judge asks, reaching up.

Horatio hands the little girl down, and the Judge takes her easily, clasping her to his chest. The girl is not much bigger than a fox. She wraps her arms around his neck, studying his face in an aloof way, like a barkeeper would a fresh-blown stranger.

'Sure is. Her given name's Talitha. But she favors Tally.'

The girl rouses a little.

'Tally is what tally does. Tally one and one is two, tally up the way to Tim-buk-tu,' she says.

'She's fit to burst with that kind of whimsy talk,' Horatio says. 'I can't figure where she picked it up from, and I got an earful on the ride up here.'

He dismounts and takes the horse by the bridle, and they walk up the hill toward the house and stable. When they reach the discarded milk pail he bends with an exhale and picks it up, as if things are now as they once were, simple as milk in the morning and the evening, and nothing more difficult than churning butter.

The Judge silently thirsts to ask about Lavinia and Plenty. He remembers them both as girls in his father-in-law's house in Louisville, bustling around on quiet feet, ironing, sewing, styling the white women's hair into ringlets and fringes and braids. They were just about his daughter, Lilah's, age. But Lilah is buried now alongside her mother in the plot by Caney Creek.

The Judge meditates, motions Horatio on to the stable, wraps the blanket more tightly around Tally, and takes her into the house. By the time Horatio comes in with the warm milk, the Judge has peeled off Tally's woolen wrappings, not a one of them a proper garment. He washes her face and hands, pulls out the straw pallet that Lilah used to sleep on out from under the bed, and tucks her under the covers. Horatio pours her a mug of milk and sits her up to drink it.

'No! Tally don't want.' The girl pushes the mug away, spilling on the blanket.

'Tally, look at this mess what you made,' Horatio says. He swipes with a grubby handkerchief at the droplets. 'Now why don't you be a good little kittycat and drink your milk?' He holds it toward her, but she clamps her mouth shut and burrows under the covers.

'Feed the spirit 'fore the flesh,' she recites neatly, muffled under her makeshift tent. Her two stiff braids peep out like antennae. The Judge, stirring the whiskey and cider in a pot over the stove and smoking, laughs softly and has to clutch at the clay pipe to keep it from falling to the floor. Horatio smiles in the guise of his old way, but doesn't show his teeth.

'Child,' he says, 'I've scraped the hidey holes of my mind to find stories enough to feed your spirit. You done cleaned me right out!'

'Have you ever heard tell of the story of God's great accident?' The Judge asks, recomposed and stuffing his pipe.

Tally uncovers herself and tucks the sheets under her chin. She shakes her head no.

'Well now,' the Judge muses, sinking into his favored chair by the fire and propping his feet up on the stone of the chimney. Horatio leans against the wall opposite the pallet.

'Undoubtedly, you've heard the creation story. Well, that's the bones of it, but they couldn't include everything in the Bible, else it would take near on forever to write, and who could stick around to get to the end of it all?'

The Judge sees that the girl is looking askance at him, and he can read the doubts in her eyes, that he's nothing but a fraud and a thief, and his story will be a droning of the same old Genesis.

'This first part will be familiar to you. In the beginning, there was God, and God was the Word, and God was with the Word. And God said, "Let there be light," and sure enough, there was light, and it was good. And then He made the stars and the earth and the land and the oceans and the plants and the critters, all the way from the teensiest gnat to the biggest whale. And all of this was good, good, good.'

The Judge sees the continued creeping suspicion over Tally's face and clears his throat.

'Now, on the sixth day, with all this landscaping and waterscaping and creating of critters, the Lord found Himself smack in the middle of a terrible mess. It was so dusty that an elephant couldn't stand without being knee-deep in the stuff. Well, God right then and there figured that before He rested up from all His work, He'd sweep the place out, give it a right good airing. And He did. He took a big old broom and descended from Heaven and started a sweeping. You never seen such a sweep. The critters went flying every which way, there was great twisters stirred up, and the debris was so thick you couldn't see a mite. When at last the dust was all swept up and God pushed it into the sea, He thought at last He could lie down and get His rest. But just as He was about to ascend back to Heaven, He got a feeling he'd never had before. It was a kind of tickling in His nose, and it worked Him up something awful, so that He thought, if He wasn't immortal, He might die right then on the spot. He heaved *ahh... ahhhh-hhhhh... CHOOOOO!* And He sneezed the first sneeze in history. Out of His nose shot a great glob of snot that landed on the earth. As it dried, it began to take form. And ever so slowly, as God Himself watched, He began to see a critter in His own image before Him. Well, He got to like the idea of something that looked like Him, so He gave it a helping hand, and thusly, out of this happy accident, this blessed sneeze, this holy snot, was created man.'

'But that's not what I heard before!' Tally declares, bolting up with eyes wide. 'And what about women folks?'

'Hush, Tally,' Horatio soothes as he eases her back onto the pillow. 'You got your story for the spirit. Now it's time for your body to sleep.'

'I know it may sound contrary to what you're used to hearing,' the Judge replies with tranquility. 'But I can assure you, I got my trusted authority that this is a real, bona fide account. Women, of course, are a different story. You'll just have to wait on that one.'

Tally huffs and turns over on the pallet, squirming and wrestling with the blankets. Horatio and the Judge glance at each other and suppress a laugh.

ADAM HUSAIN

Adam Husain graduated from the University of Oxford last year. He has written comic plays, stand-up and sketch comedy for the Edinburgh Fringe. He also edits RGBColourScheme, a small literary zine.

adamlloydhusain@gmail.com

Every Word of This is True
An extract from a novel

Katy had taken off the oversized black denim jacket that she'd borrowed from her elder brother and which I'd always hated because it was too long in the sleeves but which she thought she wore well. She wore plenty of make-up also, though you could see the crows' feet beneath her foundation; her mum had the same sort of crows' feet, although I knew that this wasn't the sort of thing you noticed if you wanted to be a good person.

'So that's it, then.'

I didn't reply, two or three times removed from the situation.

'Are you sure we shouldn't spend one last night together?'

I thought of the room we would use: a small room, with two inches of wall between us and my father's bed.

'Sorry,' I said. 'It would be too – painful.'

She nodded; Katy understood me. I rolled her off my chest to take my shirt off, then lay the shirt back down to protect my back from the grass stems. In such heat – June heat, when the sky was covered in a thick slab of cloud – the action wasn't necessarily sexual.

'You're so quiet. You've really nothing you wanted to say?'

She had looked up at me. Clearly, these were supposed to be *my last words*.

'Not really.'

The wild flowers, crushed beneath our bodies, seemed to have no scent.

'I mean, you taught me things. About how hard it is to be a woman.'

'Oh, I'm so glad I could round off your education,' Katy said.

We laughed. I licked the tears streaming down her cheeks and we laughed again. Katy rolled fully on top of me, which was sexual. Wherever they touched, our skins stuck together. She must also have been trying to make sense of these events – this 'break-up' or 'attempted break-up,' which, if it failed, would be our third attempt. I felt her up. From above, we must have looked like one creature, some kind of insect. We were kissing heavily.

We had never kissed well. I kissed with my mouth too open for Katy's taste; I kissed with my eyes open too, though sometimes she asked that I shut them to make sure I was 'in the moment,' and sometimes she would open her eyes while we were kissing, just to check.

I allowed myself an erection.

When I opened my eyes there was a black square in the corner of my vision. Almost – I didn't turn to look, but then I looked and the square moved and became a man, squatting or lying down. Katy screamed, reaching for her top; I bellowed.

'Don't mind me. Please, continue,' he said, walking towards the hedgerow.

'Who was that?'

'I think he was a birdwatcher, from the binoculars.'

'He was watching us?'

'Yeah, over there.'

We stood up after she had dressed and I found the depression his body had made in the meadow. He had been close.

'Are you all right?' I asked.

Then I asked the same question again.

I tried to work out how I ought to feel. Katy tied the denim jacket round her midriff. After all, I thought, the man had been perving on me as well.

'I want to go,' she said.

'Good idea.'

'No, *I* want to go. To Rachel's.'

'Where's that?'

'Cowley.'

'All right,' I said. 'All right, I'll walk you there.'

She wore white Reeboks and walked with both of her feet turned inwards. When we reached the turnstile, I stood on it and looked at the hedgerows. We passed through another field onto a rutted path that led past three ponies. Katy's overnight bag looked heavy. On the river, there was a group of lads trying to punt. I stopped to watch them on the footbridge.

'Got any advice?' called one.

'Nah, you're all right, mate!' I said. 'You're all right – keep going!'

Then I recomposed my face into a serious expression.

After the bridge, the path broadened and the grass on either side of it became trimmed and regular. There was a young woman walking dogs: a lab, a Dobermann, a labradoodle, a beagle, a whippet, and two springer spaniels, or they were perhaps King Charles spaniels, I can't remember. The slab of cloud had frayed in two places. Katy wore a white crop top and blue flared jeans, beneath which her shaved, white legs must have been sweaty.

'You're so quiet,' she said again.

My bike was chained to the park railings. She grabbed the handlebars when I had it free.

'Don't fuck Rebecca.'

'What? No,' I said.

We walked down a street that followed the old city wall, or perhaps it was a new wall, masquerading as the old one. There were so many things trying to look old in this city, lamb dressed up as mutton, as Mum would have said.

'You're not crying,' Katy, who was crying, said.

Before I could respond, we parted to overtake a column of French tourists, whose guide held up a pale umbrella.

'Sorry, yes.'

'You need to grow up.'

'Yes.'

'Stop saying fucking "yes"!' she said.

We crossed back over the river by a road bridge, which had some people punting beneath it though I didn't look at them.

'I'm going to block you on Facebook.'

'OK.'

'It would just be too – painful,' she said. 'And now you're smiling!'

'Am I?'

She stopped outside a red door. 'It's here.'

'We aren't really in Cowley yet.'

'I'll miss you.'

'I'll miss you too,' I said, straightening up the bike.

'What will you miss about me?'

'I'll miss everything.'

Two men walked past and eyed her.

'Hey, I'm over here,' she said.

'Sorry.'

'I love you.'

'I love you, too.'

'Bye, then.'

'Bye.'

We hugged for a while. It was a difficult thing to do, with one of my hands around her, and the other on the handlebars of the bike.

Subway smelled of artificially sweetened bread. The man ordering asked for a sandwich with one half Chipotle sauce, the other half chilli mayo, which I found impressive. I supposed I had come in here to 'treat myself', though it wasn't clear if I'd achieved anything. I thought about ordering a twelve-inch meatball sub, with Coke and cookies. The panels above the counters were a mess of green and white backlit fluorescent lights.

'What can I do you for?'

'Hi, could I have a six-inch Veggie Delight?'

'On what bread?'

'Hearty Italian.'

'With cheese on it?'

'Is it more?'

'No.'

'Then, yes.'

'And toppings?'

'All of them, please, except guac.'

I believed that the guac cost extra. The Subway bag went into the front basket of my bike. I cycled round the roundabout and over the bridge again, then hung a left, skirting down a wall behind which my sister lodged in first year, thinking herself very lucky to have an en suite – thinking she had 'lucked out', as the student helper had said at the time.

My intention was to walk into the meadows, but I sat down on the kerb after locking up the bike. My mouth was dry but I guessed that if it went cold the Subway might taste worse and so I ate it. Katy had already blocked me on Facebook, which meant that our shared photos had been erased, together with our chat on Facebook Messenger. It seemed as if I could easily have returned to the house with the red door and made it up to her, yet it wasn't clear if such an action was morally sound. Besides, it seemed then that she would call me shortly, that day or in the coming days, as she had done the two previous times.

I spent the next five weeks at my father's house. It was summer; I would hear the same tourist guides each day outside the library. I would walk with a DPhil student to get a meal deal from Boots each lunchtime at around one o'clock. The student was Indian and his accent dignified words such as 'chutney' and 'carrot cake.' On the streets, I often mistook tourists for Katy. The president of the charity was a black man, indeed an African, a fact that I felt helped to secure my project ethically. In our phone call, he told me that, alongside French, most of the inhabitants of Zè would speak Fon.

I read books on Fon culture in the library, particularly a study on *bocio*, which were the real objects that had inspired the Western myth of 'voodoo dolls.' It struck me that Katy's labia were perfect, or nearly perfect. Most *bocio* were defensive, rather than offensive, objects: wooden figures placed outside so that, instead of hurting humans, bad spirits would attack the 'doll'. The author devoted a chapter to her theory that the cords and shackles found on these *bocio* were unconscious references to the trauma of slavery, an idea which, to me, seemed a little projective, a little highly strung. I wondered if I would ever see such labia again, cycling to my father's when the library closed at ten o'clock.

It didn't seem improbable that I would at least see Katy on the streets – perhaps she would be walking from bar to bar, on towards the clubs. Perhaps she would be wearing her black, lacy bralette, beneath her black mesh top. At my father's, I microwaved a packet of quinoa, then mixed it with mayonnaise, a tin of mackerel, and garnished with some rocket. Mum called around midnight, when I had returned to work.

'Why didn't you call me?'

'I'm so sorry,' I said. 'I'm so sorry, I forgot.'

'You went out?'

'I wasn't out, Mum. Honestly, I've been working – I just forgot.'

'I haven't had dinner. We were supposed to call at eight. I waited for you. For hours, I waited. I've been waiting...'

I assured her that I did care about her and that I did love her. She told me that she had heard all that before, that words were cheap, and then she told me to ignore what she was saying because she no longer trusted her own thoughts.

'Sorry, love, I'm not seeing very well,' she said. 'I can't see things clearly at the moment.'

I told her once more that I loved her and then we hung up. It occurred to me that, in this state, I could justifiably contact Katy – but then perhaps I would be calling her partly to demonstrate that I could feel real emotions, and also that such a call could be construed as more 'emotional manipulation' if she talked about it with her friends. At the very least, I reasoned, I couldn't be in such a state as I thought I was if I'd just managed to have such a complicated sequence of thoughts.

All the same, something had to be done. My father's house was a Victorian terraced house built for canal workers. Most likely, the neighbours could hear me sobbing through the walls.

SHEREEN JACKSON

Shereen Jackson is this year's recipient of the UEA BAME crowdfunded scholarship. She holds a BA in Hispanic Studies with English Literature from King's College London. Shereen is working on a collection of short stories that depict the quiet discomfort of everyday life. She also has a novel in progress, *Origitorigi,* which follows the lives of children growing up in rural Norfolk.

shereen_jackson@hotmail.com

Everything is Fine
A short story

I glance at my wife. Pretty but too skinny, she worries about her weight. She is overdressed for a heatwave. Silk blouse, flowing skirt, freckled face hidden beneath a straw hat. We are walking on the Heath, just before the incline becomes Parliament Hill. The city in the summer is a treasure trove of skin. Hips, breasts, legs, elbows, ankles, tans, birthmarks, clavicles. I look. I get lost. I remember summer romances, illicit kisses; girls in minis, in bikinis; unchartered flesh.

Our children run ahead, wispy figures in the long grass, their skin white with sun cream. Laura finds a place in the shade and arranges our elaborate picnic on a chequered sheet, as if we are at a banquet. Her movements are perfectly orchestrated. I think back to when a packet of crisps, torn open to reveal the salty insides, with a shot of anything alcoholic, would have sufficed. Now it's co-ordinated picnicware, juice cartons for the boys, chilled wine for us and a sharp knife to slice the cheese; she's even brought a chopping board.

Laura cuts the cheddar and Camembert into neat, little rectangles and displays them like flattened tombstones on a plastic plate. After hauling the picnic to the Heath, I am hot and breathless. I'd love a cold Sol but Laura forgot to pack the beer, even though I reminded her this morning. A jazz quartet plays on the bandstand. Laura hums along. She photographs the picnic tableau for her Instagram page and calls out to the boys. They settle on the blanket and moan about the lack of ham and crisps. They pick at their cheese and avocado sandwiches. Laura promises ice cream for dessert.

As we eat, a different type of music drifts up the hill. A group of youngsters is headed our way. They are tanned and glittered and look like they've been up all night. One of them carries a speaker plugged into their phone. I don't recognise the song. They walk up the hill, laughing, jostling, talking incessantly. They must be on drugs, but what kind? Cocaine, ecstasy, speed? We no longer do this, Laura and I. We have moved on. We are hard-working, law-abiding, clean-living.

I watch the group. I smell their weed. They must be... eighteen, nineteen, good-looking with tattoos, edgy haircuts, and shiny jewellery. There is a girl with long, dark hair. Her body is soft, generous. She wears a feathered crown and a flimsy playsuit. A boy walks with her, his arm slung around her shoulders. He licks her neck. The girl laughs.

The group drops their belongings onto the ground. They sit close enough for it to feel like an intrusion.

'Do you want to move?' I ask Laura.

'Don't be silly,' she replies and lies down with the papers. I finish my sandwich and gulp down the wine. I scan the Travel supplement and read an article about spas in Mexico. Every now and then I glance at the group. The boy and girl touch each other through their clothes; she is sitting in his lap. She grinds against him, laughing.

'Dad! Ice cream!' Jake and Freddie shout.

'All right,' I say and pick them up, one under each arm like barrels of beer. My muscles flex beneath my T-shirt. I have been working out. The boys wriggle and shout. I put them down and we walk down the hill. Laura has stayed behind to have 'five minutes peace and quiet.' We take a detour to the toilets before heading to buy the ice creams. The queue to the van is ridiculous and we stand in the heat for a long time.

'How much longer?' the boys whine.

We start moving when I spot the dark-haired girl and her boyfriend at the front of the queue. The girl hands over her money and the boyfriend reaches for their ice creams. He has curly black hair, a silver stud in one ear. He turns. His eyes wander and then settle on us. Or is he looking at someone else? He walks the length of the queue towards us. His girlfriend has fallen behind; she is trying to shove her purse inside a handbag shaped like a pineapple. The boy is getting closer. He brushes past.

'Pervert,' he whispers. He stands very close. I can smell the booze, his sweat.

'I saw you.' He nods towards his girlfriend. 'Watching *her*.'

'What?' I circle my arms around the boys, bringing them close.

'You heard me.' His girlfriend arrives. She looks at me and bites the end of the Flake in her 99 cone.

Close up, I see that she is young, *too* young, fifteen or sixteen. She isn't even pretty. I look away. I stare directly at the ice cream van.

'Dad?' Jake, my eldest, tugs at my T-shirt. I place a hand on the side of his head, to reassure him. I let my hand slip to his ear and press his head against my hip. He doesn't need to hear this. Jake has an ear for drama, a talent for telling tales. Freddie makes crying noises until I shush him. I look at the teenage boy.

'You're crazy,' I say. I shuffle forwards. The queue is moving, slowly.

'Fuck!' The boy shakes his head. 'I know what I saw. Fucking paedo.'

He gives me the finger. Several people in the line turn and stare. The teenage boy walks away, grabbing his girlfriend's hand. They take the hill in strides. I hear them laughing. My skin itches in the heat. I release my hand from Jake's ears and give both boys a cuddle.

'Dad?' Jake asks again.

I look straight ahead. I say, 'Don't worry about it.'

We reach the front of the queue and I buy the boys a Cornetto and one for Laura too, even though I know she doesn't like ice cream. When we walk back, I avoid looking at the group.

Laura has been dozing. She sits up and her hat tumbles onto the blanket. Her red-blonde hair spills over her freckled shoulders and she smiles. When we were young, I would count the freckles on her body until the counting became infinite. I offer her the half-melted ice cream. She shakes her head.

'You know I don't eat ice cream,' she says.

I slurp some of the Cornetto. It's sweet and sickly. I chuck the rest into a plastic bag. Jake sits by his mother; Freddie paws at her, asking for cuddles.

'What's wrong?' Laura asks, sitting Freddie in her lap. She strokes Jake's hair. Neither he nor Freddie answer. Laura looks at me.

'Nothing,' I say. 'Everything's fine.'

I lie down to read the paper. I finish the bottle of wine. The sky above is blue and cloudless and the sun warms my skin. I drop the paper and close my eyes. I'm not sure how long I sleep but when I wake up, Laura and the boys are no longer beside me. I can hear their voices; their laughter. They are playing frisbee a few metres away. I turn to lie on my front and watch the game unfold. In the distance, the teenagers are dancing; arms and hips moving in a tribal way, eyes closed against the sun. The boy and the girl are kissing. Their kisses probably taste of sugar.

Laura and the boys have never played frisbee before. I am surprised at how good they are. Freddie is six but more athletic than his older brother; he hurls the frisbee in the air. It spins past Laura, arches towards the teenagers and lands by their feet. The frisbee hasn't hit anyone but Laura races over, already apologising. I sit up. The girl with dark hair picks up the frisbee but her boyfriend takes it and walks towards Laura. I watch as the boy hands her the frisbee. They speak. I feel the wine curdle in my stomach. I stand up and begin to tidy away the picnic. Laura and the boy continue to talk. Finally, she walks away with the frisbee in her hand. She reaches Jake and Freddie and puts her arms around them. She smiles. I exhale quickly. Nothing is wrong. I finish packing up the picnic. Laura and the boys walk back.

'What are you doing?' Laura asks. Her cheeks are flushed.

'It's getting late.'

She looks at the silver watch on her wrist. 'It's only two.'

'Right,' I say. 'But maybe we should go? I have work to do before tomorrow.' I turn to the boys. I smile at Freddie. 'Great frisbee playing, Fred.'

'Did you see how far it went?' he asks, grinning. I nod. I look at Laura carefully. Her face seems neutral, normal.

'OK,' she says. 'Let's go.'

We pick up our things and walk down the hill in pairs: Freddie with me, Jake with his mother. I don't look at the group as we walk past. I talk to Freddie about the rules of cricket, which I have promised to play on our next visit to the Heath. Laura and Jake walk behind us. Every now and then I glance back. I see Laura stop to hug Jake. Freddie and I keep walking and talking, and when I look back Laura and Jake are still standing there, hugging.

'Everything OK?' I shout.

They unwrap their arms and stare at me. They nod and start walking. When we reach the car park, Laura reminds the boys not to run behind the cars. She reaches into her purse for the keys and releases the central locking system. I load our bags into the boot. When I finish, Laura is standing, watching me. The boys haven't got into the car; Freddie is picking at a scab on his elbow and Jake is tapping away at his mother's phone.

'Aren't you getting in?' I ask.

Laura nods. 'Yes. I'll drive. You've had too much to drink.'

'Fine,' I say. 'I'll see you out.'

I stand away from the car whilst Laura and the boys get in. Laura starts the engine. I beckon her, indicating that it is safe for her to reverse. I swivel my index finger so she knows to turn her wheels. The wheels turn sharply and she backs the car out quickly.

'Whoa, whoa,' I say and make the stop sign. She continues reversing and I have to jump out of the way. The car stops, moves forward and then stops again. I walk towards it, my heart beating quickly.

'Bloody hell!' I say with my hand on the roof of the car, my head close to the open window. Laura frowns. She grips the steering wheel with both hands.

'You should walk home,' she says, not looking at me.

'What?'

'I think it would be best.'

'I don't...'

'We can talk once you're home.'

'Talk about what?'

'I'm not stupid, Damon,' she says. She slams her foot on the accelerator and drives away. I fumble in my pocket for my phone. I call Laura but she doesn't pick up. I call again and again until finally, she answers.

'Dad?' Jake says.

'Jake, put Mummy on.'

There is a muffled sound and I hear Laura's voice, terse but faint, in the background. I can't hear what she is saying. After a minute Jake comes back on. 'Mummy says... Mummy says she can't talk now because she is driving. She says you should walk home.'

I hear Freddie's voice in the background. 'Can we play frisbee when you get home, Daddy?'

'Quiet, Freddie!' Jake orders, in a voice much like his mother's. Then he says, 'Bye Dad. See you soon.'

I don't respond. There is a short silence and then Freddie's high-pitched voice fills the void. 'Bye Daddeeee,' he says. 'You silly-billy-silly-billy-silly-billy.'

NOZIZWE CYNTHIA JELE

Nozizwe Cynthia Jele is a South African author. Her debut novel, *Happiness is a Four-Letter Word* (Kwela Books, 2010), won the Best First Book category (Africa region) in the Commonwealth Writers' Prize 2011. The book was adapted into a film with the same title. *The Ones with Purpose* (Kwela Books, 2018), her second novel, was longlisted for the International Dublin Literary Prize 2020.

info@nozizwecynthiajele.com
https://nozizwecynthiajele.com
@jelecynthia

Platinum Tupperware
An excerpt from a novel

After breakfast, Shadrach pulls his car out of the garage into the driveway, the 2007 Mercedes-Benz E350 Elegance, steady and reliable after all these years. He leaves the engine idle, door open, walks around the car, inspecting the windscreen for chips, the thread on the wiper blades, double-checks the licence disc expiry date, and lightly kicks the tyres as he has done every morning the car has been on duty. He opens the rear passenger door and checks the satchel of sealed fabric softener he keeps under the seat; if there is one thing he has learned from the years of driving, it is that a smooth drive and a fresh-smelling car makes the ride. It is the reason why he never eats or sleeps in his car, because who knows how long a fart lingers on the seats? He moves to the driver's side and checks the leather holster mounted under the dashboard. He finds the firearm, a 9mm Parabellum, where he had left it.

When he is satisfied with his ten-point inspection, he goes back inside the house. He finds his daughter, Lusanda, in the kitchen standing near the opened fridge, scrutinising its half-empty contents. There is an open notebook on the tabletop where she has scribbled a few items – eggs, yogat, carrots, cheese, chicken, wors, russians, cold drinks (Stoney ginger beer) – in neat cursive writing, which she will lose in a few years, deeming it old-fashioned and unnecessary.

'You've spelled yoghurt incorrectly.'

'Oh?' Lusanda glances over at her writing. 'But it says yogat.'

'That's not how you write it.' Shadrach spells out the correct word to his daughter.

'That doesn't make sense,' she protests.

'We don't make the rules. The owners of the language decide what goes.'

He watches her draw a straight line over the incorrect word and rewrite it. He is learning to do right by this one, to be 'present' in all possible forms; as he had overhead one of his passengers scream down their phone a couple of years back, before abruptly ending their call.

'Men are full of shit,' the passenger said. 'Do you have kids, umh...?'

'Shadrach. Yes, twin boys, at varsity, and a little girl.'

'Are you present in their lives? I mean r-e-a-l-l-y present?' She stretched out the word as if spelling it out, 'as in, know their birthdays, teachers they least like, class averages, names of their best friends? Because there is a difference, Meshach, in being a father who happened to donate a sperm and a r-e-a-l father. A huge difference. This is what I'm trying to explain to my husband, that it's unacceptable for him to assign all the parenting responsibilities to me. You know what that son of a bitch does? Hides behind work. Oh, yes, he does. Anyway...' She had sighed and looked out the window. 'I'm tired of the bullshit. You can drop me off at the gate. How much do I owe you? Do you take cash? Do well by your kids and their mother. Be p-r-e-s-e-n-t.'

'Dad?'

Shadrach looks down at his daughter who is watching him with curiosity. 'Yes, Lu. Where is Mama?'

'In your room.'

He starts towards their bedroom but, hearing her voice, stops halfway across the lounge. 'Yes, he is starting today... No, he's not ready but he will not listen, you know how stubborn he gets. Honestly, I'm not prepared to deal with that again... If he wants to work himself to the grave he must do so without involving us... Traumatic experience I don't wish on my worst enemy... Try to tell him that... Tired...' He traces his steps backwards until he is in the kitchen. 'Well, I'm off,' he says not necessarily loudly.

'Bye Dad,' Lusanda says. 'Don't forget your mask.'

From his house on Limpopo Street, Shadrach joins Zuurfontein Road and heads south where he will join the highway to take him to the suburb of Morningside in Sandton. The traffic is moderate at this time with the morning rush subsided; he has enough time before his pick-up. He thinks about the unexpected call and how it had lifted his mood. The business with Phindile had nearly spoiled his day. How could his heart let him down at such a crucial moment? It was not a pain he felt, no, more like a spasm from the chest muscles but it had scared the hell out of him. He hasn't been on this road since they operated on him. He rolls down the car windows letting in the morning breeze. The street noise is bearable at this time of the day, before the minibus taxis and street vendors dominate. After driving for about two kilometres, he turns left and stops at his friend's tuckshop. The Coca-Cola sponsored signage, Tebzas Grocery & Hot Foods, hangs above the shop. Teboho 'Tebza' Malope is standing behind the serving hatch facing the street. He buzzes open the security gate at the entrance when he sees Shadrach.

'Shadow, my friend, what a surprise. What a surprise. Come in, come in.' He opens the side door of the shop and ushers him in. 'I don't believe it, come here… No, can't do that. A jab then. Man, good to see you.'

'How is this our lives? I can't wait for this nightmare to be over.'

'We are all over it.'

A moment passes.

'I didn't expect you back on the road so soon. You're not going to work, are you?' Teboho looks at him, concerned. 'Did Phindile agree to this?'

'Please, not you too. I'm taking it easy, a few hours, keeping it local. I miss the road.'

A child is at the gate. Teboho buzzes him in. He greets the child and asks after his parents' and grandparents' health. The child gives a one-word answer: fine. He asks for a loaf of white bread and a small bag of atchaar. Teboho adds a piece of candy to his purchases. The child's eyes sparkle.

'Thank you, Uncle Teboho,' the child says, and leaves.

'Just you today?' Shadrach asks, looking around.

'The girls are with their grandmother this weekend. They need it. I've given the helper time off before I'm accused of being a slave driver.'

'Listen, my friend. I am sorry I couldn't be there for you. I loved Maggie like she was my sister.'

'Thank you, I know you would have been here if circumstances were different. What can we say, when it's time, it's time. I take pleasure knowing she didn't suffer in the end.'

'We are at war with the virus.'

'And our leaders do not seem to care.' His voice trails. 'But enough of the sadness. We have much to be grateful for.'

No one says anything for a moment.

'I see you've beefed up security. Did they try to…? Did something happen?'

Teboho points to the remnants of a burnt wall, parts of which have been repainted and covered with more brands signage. 'They attempted to burn the shop when they found out I had provided shelter to three Somalis who operate a mini-supermarket by the clinic. We managed to douse the fire before it spread.'

'Jesus, Tebza. No one was hurt? I wasn't aware.'

He shakes his head. 'You have to nurse your heart to health, you don't need to concern yourself with all the stresses of the world. I asked your wife not to tell you, no one was hurt and the damage was minimal.'

'Shouldn't have happened.'

'I'm not even angry at the people. We're turning on each other because we're frustrated. People are hungry. Best we can do is try to protect ourselves. Look here, do you know what this is?' Teboho shows Shadrach a box, no larger than a small cellphone. 'These young chaps came and installed a wireless motion sensor with long-term battery life and a 100-decibel siren. You go deaf if that thing is triggered.' He explains how the alarm is linked to the community police forum members. 'I tell you, this technology is the one. I can sleep a little better at night.'

'This is your livelihood, your only source of income. Just because they are hungry or frustrated with the ruling party does not give them the right to take what does not belong to them. There is a line between protest and criminality.'

'That is a debate for another day, my friend. For now, let's celebrate life or whatever is left of it for us.'

Inside the shop, a single-car converted garage, the air is thick with the smells of cooking oil and fabric softener. The whirly emits a constant buzzing; Teboho has turned on the fan. The shelves are stocked to the brim with miniature soap boxes, cooking oils, cans of baked beans, and pilchards. An entire side of the shops is filled with bottles of sanitisers of varying sizes and disposable and cloth masks in single and multiple packs.

'Soon you will be selling the vaccine, my friend,' Shadrach comments.

'Don't joke, you know I have cold storage at the back.'

'I know. Anyway, I better be off. Give me three vetkoeks, water, and a cigarette. I need a sniff to prepare me for the day.'

Teboho moves towards the double door cooler, takes out a bottle of water and hands it to Shadrach. 'This you can have.'

'Come on, soon I'll turn into a garden. All I've been eating is leaves and leaves. How much chicken and fish can a man eat? I need something solid to line my stomach. You should see my lunch box.'

'You nearly died,' Teboho says.

'It's over now. Look at me. Now be good and give me my food, add a thick slice of polony while you're at it.'

'Just this once and only because I'm happy to see you.' Teboho opens a yellow bucket on the table next to the cash machine and with a tong, takes out vetkoeks and puts them in a sandwich bag. He adds a slice of polony. From his shirt pocket, he pulls out a box of cigarettes and hands it to Shadrach, who takes two.

Shadrach searches his pockets for his wallet but Teboho stops him.

'It's on the house.'

'You will run out of business giving friends freebies.'

'How is your Phindile and Lusanda?'

'Good, great. Phindile is moving her company to a warehouse in Wynberg. Her funding application was approved yesterday.'

'You have to admit it, my friend, you got lucky with that woman.'

'Careful now,' Shadrach laughs.

'Seriously, man, the woman is a born entrepreneur. Everything she touches turns into gold. Remember when she quit at Checkers to focus on her business? We thought she was mad to leave. But she proved us wrong, look at her now, from chopping and packing fruit and vegetables on her kitchen table to owning her warehouse. That's progress.'

Shadrach shrugs. He makes out to say something, stops.

Teboho pats his shoulder. 'You have nothing to worry about. It's her time to shine. Be part of her success.'

'Yeah, Tebza. Listen, let me move,' Shadrach walks towards the door, to the small yard. 'Thank you for padkos.'

'Your birthday next weekend, are we doing anything?'

'The wife won't hear of anything that involves more than the family. I know we can't take our guard off the virus and there's talk of a third wave, but we also need to live. We could all do with a small celebration. I've missed seeing people and we've lost many.'

'Don't push it, man.'

Shadrach tries not to think of his wife as he places the sandwich bag next to the lunch box of carefully packed leftover dinner. From Teboho's, Shadrach returns to the main road. He swerves around the debris of a building that caught fire during the last protest. He wishes the speed of development in his township would move beyond this constipated phase. The change in leadership has not brought about any changes; politicians are the same whether dressed in gold or red or blue.

He follows the stretch of the road until the Grayston Drive fork which takes him over the M1 highway, passing the pedestrian and cycling bridge to his left which joins their humble neighbourhood to Africa's richest square mile. The centre of Sandton rises before him to his left, the newly constructed The Leonardo piercing the blue sky. He has watched these glass and steel structures pop up, one after the other, rearranging the landscape of his childhood. A minibus taxi cuts in front of him only to stop a few metres away to drop off a passenger. Shadrach applies the brakes and changes lanes.

ROSE KEATING

Rose Keating is an Irish writer who has been published in *Banshee*, *Southword*, the *Honest Ulsterman*, and *Hot Press* magazine. She is the winner of the Marian Keyes Young Writer Award and the Hot Press Write Here Write Now prize. She is a recipient of the Malcolm Bradbury Memorial Scholarship.

rosekeating729@gmail.com

Eggshells
A short story

She felt her stomach cramp as the egg began to move downwards.

Sunrise leaked through the curtains, shadows blushing. Beside her, Luke's sleep-sour breath, soft on her cheek. She took the lube out of the side desk. She poured a cool, clear dollop on her palm, pulled down her underwear and held her labia apart. The folds were dry and sensitive, and when she began to massage the lube in, she felt the tender skin recoil at the cold shock.

'Do you want me to help?' Luke said, voice small. His erection pressed against her thigh.

'No.' She tried to press her fingers in deeper but it was sore, the stiff muscle tensing as the cramps grew.

'What if it cracks again?'

'Please go back to sleep.'

'You woke me. I'm just trying to help.'

'I don't need help.' She removed her slick fingers from her hole, wiping them on the blanket.

The egg was coming; she grimaced at the building pressure. She pushed hard, clenching her fists. Her muscles spasmed and then the egg was moving through her, slipping down the walls of her cunt. The egg was full and firm but the stretch mostly painless.

'Don't forget to catch it,' Luke said. Lisa rolled her eyes and moved her hand just below her opening. A moment later, the egg popped out with a small squelch, dropping into her palm.

The egg was a light tan, speckled with brown freckles. It glistened in the early morning light, drooling with lube. The greased shell felt warm as blood.

'It's getting on the blanket,' Luke said. She stood and placed the egg in the incubation box opposite the bed.

'Did you do your positive associations last night?' he asked.

She thought about not answering.

'You should go,' she said.

She heard his silence, then rustling sheets. She tapped the egg with her finger. His lips on her shoulder. Brief, dry. 'I'll text you,' he said.

She showered and dressed. After, she checked the incubation box, removing the lid.

The shell lay in splinters. In the corner of the transparent box, a fish thrashed, bashing its tail against the side. It was pink and had grown larger than the egg it had hatched from. When it saw her looking, it stilled. It lifted its neck and it smiled, its mouth filled with large, square teeth.

'You piece of shit,' it said. Its breath smelled of cloves.

She hummed and stooped, checking for abnormalities. Instead of scales, a layer of skin, rosy as a newborn. One eye missing, three extra fins on its belly. She grabbed her phone and input the info into her cycle app. She put the lid back on and left for the call centre.

—

She came home late. The box was spattered with yolk. The hatchling lay unmoving. She sponged the box clean then disposed of the hatchling and shell, dropping them into the kitchen compost bin. She rinsed the dirtied sponge under the sink, watching the water run gold.

She opened Luke's texts and waited seventy minutes to reply. He arrived within ten minutes, a loaf of bread cradled in the crook of his arm, rocking it back and forth.

'I made it myself,' he said, beaming.

'I'll bet.' She took the bread and put it on the counter.

She had him get on his knees and eat her out at the kitchen table. She yanked at the roots of his hair and called him a good boy and let him cry against her leg after he came in his pants. He pressed his forehead into her knee, snot-nosed and panting. Eventually, he stood.

'I should go.' His eyes were red, his mouth swollen. He wiped his nose with the back of his hand and stared at a spot on the floor.

'Cool!' she said. She walked him to the door.

Before she went to sleep that night, she found a podcast for guided associations. She pressed play and closed her eyes.

'Imagine a small, white cat,' the guide whispered. 'Imagine its fur on your skin. It is good, and clean, and it is yours. You are good, and clean, and your body is yours. You are in control. Imagine the cat. The cat is beautiful. You are capable of beautiful things.'

The cat that emerged from the egg on Tuesday morning didn't have eyes. There were no sockets for eyes to grow in, just a furry flat plane on the top half of its face. It made a whining noise when she opened the lid. Lisa reached down to stroke it. The fur was matted and infested with lice. It purred when she stroked it, but then it let out a low, masculine moan. She withdrew her hand and the cat chuckled. 'Luke is as good as it gets,' it said.

She forgot to listen to the guide that night but did watch *The Phantom of the Opera* (2004). On Wednesday morning the egg cracked and hundreds of flies emerged, swarming the box. They were lavender and collectively buzzed out the melody of 'Angel of Music'.

She clapped when they finished. All at once their wings fell off and they dropped out of the air. One of the flies crawled to the glass and shook a tiny fist at her.

'Your mam feels alone all the time,' the fly said. 'She is afraid to go to shops because of large crowds. Her heating broke and she is very cold and you told her you'd get someone to fix it but you didn't. Her tits sag to her belly button and their heavy weight hurts her back and sometimes when she looks in the mirror she starts crying. You never call. She thinks about how you never call. She thinks about it all the time.'

She called Mam that evening. Mam told her about Pat from next door who had fixed her heating and about every member of the parish who had recently died. Lisa half listened, thinking about how she was going to tell Mam she loved her. 'Are you seeing anyone?' Mam asked.

'No.'

'Pat's single.'

'OK.'

'How are your eggs? Are they still regular?'

'They're fine.'

'Any abnormalities? Are you keeping up with the positive associations?'

'Mam.'

'I'm only asking. It's important at your age.'

'Yeah. I've got to go, Mam.' Lisa waited to hear Mam's goodbye and then hung up.

She texted Luke asking him to come over. For twenty minutes the icon showed her that Luke was typing. She turned off her phone and went to bed.

She was late for work the next morning and lay the egg as quickly as she could, straining her muscles. She tried to piss after it was in the box. She noticed drops of blood in the bowl; it had been awhile since she had ripped anything.

She returned to her bedroom. Inside the box sat a baby.

Lisa touched her stomach. 'I'm not pregnant,' she said.

'No, I'm not a real baby. Just a hatchling, don't worry!' he said. He had a crisp, rich accent, like a presenter on the news.

'Oh, that's good.' Lisa sat down on the bed, looking at the box. The baby smiled at her. He tried to sit up but his head lolled to the side, unable to hold its weight.

'Can I come out?' he asked.

'I don't think I'm meant to. It's bad for cycles.'

'You're probably infertile. And you'd be a terrible mother. You're a bad person. You are deeply selfish and fundamentally lacking in the generosity and depth of character needed to love another. So, you may as well.' The baby winked.

She took him out. He was a beautiful baby, blemish free, but his skin was sticky with yolk and left a slimy layer on her fingers.

She lay back down in bed, holding him in her arms. 'I don't even like children,' she said. The baby hummed and nuzzled into her chest. His skin left a yellow stain on the white of her pyjama top.

'That's not really the point though, is it?'

'No,' she said. She realised the baby's movements were growing slower. He cocked a fair eyebrow at her.

'Want to put me back in the box?'

She shook her head. He gurgled and grabbed at her hand, beaming. She let him clutch at her finger. Eventually, his grip relaxed.

She lay there for longer than she should have then went to work, leaving the hatchling in the bed.

For the first hour, she felt fine. In the second, she felt lightheaded. Her stomach began to cramp while on a call. She took a breath as the pain hit her abdomen. She closed her eyes, focusing on her breathing. The pain shifted lower as she listened to the customer's complaint.

She felt a pressure in her groin. Her eyes snapped open as she realised what was happening. She stood, dropping the phone. She took a step, hoping to get to the toilets, then she felt something crack.

She froze. She looked down at her crotch. The grey of her trousers had darkened. In the wet patch yolk seeped through, gold globs oozing down her inner thigh.

'Lisa,' someone whispered.

Someone laughed and someone else made a hushing sound. Someone sighed; it sounded like her mother.

Her manager called her into his office. 'This is very inappropriate,' he said. 'I mean, in public. Really, Lisa.'

'I didn't mean to. I already had one this morning.'

'Oh. Is this, uh,' he said. He clicked his pen and looked down at his desk. 'Usual? For you?'

'Why?'

'If you're feeling unwell, management should know. We're here to support the mental health of our employees. Positive mind, positive eggs, all that.'

She stared at him. He continued to look down at the pen, clicking it rapidly.

'Fantastic,' she said. 'I'm fantastic.'

She turned to leave and felt the crunch of a piece of shell inside her as she moved.

—

She finally opened Luke's texts. The word 'aftercare' was used, the word 'unfair', the word 'selfish'. Then there were several apologies, a plea to come over, a picture of his erect cock. She sent a thumbs up. She cleaned up the box and disposed of the hatchling.

She stayed up all night watching YouTube compilations of positive eggs. Fat, large-eyed rabbits, quivering tails on rounded rumps as plump and soft as a fuzzy peach. More ambitious creations: sleeping unicorns the size of teacups, miniature dragons with flames that blew no hotter than a mellow summer breeze.

'It's all about focus,' one of the women said, holding the dragon on her palm. 'Self-control. Positivity. Not that hard!' She laughed as the dragon did a cartwheel around her fingers.

She didn't realise it was morning until she felt the cramp. She considered soiling herself. Instead, she took out the lube and began to prep. Pieces of shell from the last egg were still inside her. She picked them out gently. The yolk had dried on the folds of her vulva and smelled rich and sour.

When the egg was out and in the incubation box, she got a make-up wipe from the bathroom. She wiped the yolk from her crotch and then came back to check the box.

The egg was split down in the middle in two halves, unnaturally symmetrical, and the box was empty.

She lifted the egg, dipping a finger in. The shell was dry, fragile, and entirely clean of yolk. She pressed the halves against her cheek, feeling for warmth.

She rang Mam while clutching the egg. It went to voicemail. She decided to leave a message. After the beep, she tried to remember what she had wanted to say. She got back into bed. She tucked the egg in with her and pressed the phone against her ear. She curled close to the shell and closed her eyes as the message recorded, breathing into the warm, static dark of the voicemail.

DEREK KEOGH

Derek Keogh was born in Tipperary. He is working on a short story collection that focuses on the negative space, and the seemingly innocuous events that build to significant and sometimes overwhelming ones. One of his stories has been published in *The Stinging Fly* magazine.

derekkeogh@gmail.com

The Will
An extract from a short story

The drive back from the funeral is slow. The roads are wet and every town Darren drives through is congested with traffic. For the last fifteen miles of the journey, he gets stuck behind a tractor hauling large tubular bales of hay wrapped in black plastic, and throwing up, from its tyres, brown muck from the road which splatters his windscreen. Darren has run out of wiper fluid and stays well back to keep from muddying up his visibility. His eyes narrow with the strain of the drive and the three days he has been away.

Shaking out the stiffness of the car journey, Darren tousles with the rusted padlock while Shep licks his hands through the railings of the gate. He jiggles the lock violently and a russet of dust spills from its innards as it yields to the key. Shep backs up a pace, gives two shrill barks, circles around and barks again, his tail slicing through the air.

'Calm down, boy. Calm down.'

The house is cold and smells of untreated rising damp, and the sense that it has not been lived in for longer than a few days. Darren hangs his cap on a nail inside the door, removes the key from above the grandfather clock and winds it, tipping the pendulum into motion before moving the hands to the right time.

In the kitchen, he rakes the cinders and ash, and stuffs the empty grate with balled newspaper. Darren splits kindling with a hand axe and stacks it around the paper, then puts a match to it and watches. Once the fire takes, he adds a few sods of turf and a shovel of coal.

Darren removes his good shoes without stooping, leveraging the heel of one off with the toe of the other, and slips his feet into the army-green wellies standing sentry by the door. He takes his cap and whistles.

'Come on, boy. We'll go for a walk while the house warms up.'

—

The boreen that crosses Darren's land is quiet except for the noise of his own footfall. Shep scampers ahead on the grass verge that runs along the centre. The air is heavy with moisture the rain shower failed to clear. Darren inhales and welcomes the familiar scent of the land.

The hedgerow is bare of leaves with only a scattering of berries clinging on. He recalls foraging for these berries with his uncle on weekend trips to the farm, returning with Co-op shopping bags filled to the brim for his grandmother. She had a homemade preventive cure for all seasonal ailments: wild mushrooms boiled in creamy milk with lashings of pepper to line the stomach and keep out infections; rose hip and haw preserves to fight off bugs; roasted horse chestnuts with a cross scored on the top, nature's communion, to take down any swelling; and to prevent a chest infection, an acrid tea brewed from pine needles. His uncle would joke that it had to be good for you, for it tasted like medicine, though he enjoyed the sweet smell of berries on the boil as much as the rest of them.

Darren looks beyond the hedgerow, to the acres of tillage stretching to the horizon in one direction, running up to the base of the forested hills that wrap around, and down, to the soggy plains of bogland. Out there, during the War of Independence, Darren's grandfather and others from the community lowered rifles into sinkholes in the bog to hide them from the British. The Tans scoured the land, the officers insisting they were there somewhere. They stood no chance of finding them though, unless they happened to fall in on top, and if they did, they were never seen or heard from again. There were no man-made markers, you had to know the land, and they could only be located by a triangulation of the tussocks of wild grass. The remains of the neighbour that informed on them still lies at the bottom of one of the sinkholes. Darren's uncle often pointed out the very one.

Men on the run would come to the back door, where they were fed and hidden in the forest until it was safe to move on. Darren never met his grandfather, or the countless others whose stories attached them to the land, but he felt them whenever he walked the lane.

A throng of cattle rounds the bend at a pace. Darren steps down into a ditch and whistles. Shep's head whips around. Darren slaps his hand on his thigh twice and Shep loops back and settles by his feet. The cows scurry past, their fur caked with dry manure and mottled with bald patches. Darren removes his cap and runs his palm back over the smooth crown of his head.

Following close behind is a new Massey Ferguson with the loader at half-height and the throttle racing high. It stops alongside Darren and the door swings open.

'It's a grand evening,' Keir says, looking down on Darren.

'Changeable enough.'

The sheepdog in the cabin lurches at the window, barking and snapping at Shep. Keir gives him a blow to the ribcage with his work-swollen fingers. 'Shut up,' he shouts. The dog yelps and folds down into the footwell of the tractor.

At Darren's side, Shep whines. He dances his fingers along Shep's head and snout.

'I heard you were away for a few days,' Keir says.

'An old neighbour passed. I'd to pay my respects.'

'Wasn't too sudden, I hope.'

'Sudden enough in the end, as is usually the case. Though she made it into her eighties.'

'Ah, nothing to complain about there then. Nature taking its course.'

'Few of us greet it when it comes, all the same.' Darren looks at the splattered cow dung along the lane with the fresh tyre tracks running through it. The silence becomes uneasy.

'Not much left of the evenings now with the clocks gone back,' Keir says, reaching for conversation.

'No, nothing but long dark nights ahead of us now.'

'I'd better be getting the milking done before the day is gone on me.' Keir starts the tractor. 'I'll call up to the house one of these days and we can have a word.'

Darren salutes and stays in the ditch watching the tractor speed up on the slowing herd.

Try as he might, Darren cannot recapture his earlier mood as he continues along the lane. The unexpected encounter with Keir has pushed the stories of the land from his mind and made way for thoughts of his visit to St Luke's in Dublin on the way to the funeral.

Doctor Doyle had been urging Darren to go for a scan ever since his first appointment. Darren had not been feeling himself for months and held to the notion that he'd come down with a bug that he couldn't shake. The mere sight of food turned his stomach and what he did manage to eat seemed to wash right through him. Darren hoped it would pass but when the traces of maroon appeared in the toilet bowl, he rang for an appointment. Doctor Doyle said the scan was nonintrusive and only a precautionary measure to help eliminate another thing from the list. Darren resisted saying it wouldn't be worth a trip specially, though aware he couldn't put it off for too long. He knew the result the scan would yield. The mind can lie, but the body knows its own truth.

So, when Darren got word that Kitty had passed, he called Doctor Doyle who made the necessary arrangements. He was to be there at ten o'clock on the Friday morning and all he needed to do in preparation was to skip breakfast.

The smell of the hospital alone was enough to make Darren close in on himself and he immediately contemplated leaving. The young woman on reception must have seen this in his face, for she stepped from behind the counter and walked him to the radiology department. She enquired if Darren had travelled far and he laughed and asked if it was that obvious that he was an outsider. She blushed, and Darren quickly said that he'd just come down from Cavan and talked about the state of the roads.

She handed him over to a nurse, mock-threatening her to take good care of him, then went back along the corridor with a cheerio. Darren felt belittled by her performance, though he appreciated the effort all the same.

The radiology nurse was busy, with a practised, casual manner. She handed him a gown and pointed to a room where he was to slip the gown on and she'd call for him in a jiffy.

Lying in the core of the magnetic cylinder with a padded coil on his stomach, Darren thought about his childhood trips to the farm, and his parents' efforts to make sure he never missed one. His sister Kathy and brother Martin were given a choice, and they seldom went, and never during school term. Darren was never permitted an excuse. Even if he had reams of homework that he couldn't possibly finish, the trip still went ahead and a note was written for school. In over forty years he never made the connection until it came to him there, flat on his back, with a giant magnet cranking and thumping around him: his parents knew all along the farm had to go to someone and they'd positioned him for the windfall.

The aroma of frying sausages and rashers permeates the kitchen. Shep's ears lift; he rises and barks. The latch of the outer door opens, followed by the sound of boots being kicked against the wall. Shep's ears and tail slacken, though he remains poised. The kitchen door opens cautiously and Peter's head pops around.

'Did I catch you at a bad time?'

'Not at all. Come in.' Darren lifts the frying pan from the heat and sets it aside. He covers the fire with the metal lid.

'You're about to eat. I'll come back.' Peter steps into the kitchen and closes the door.

'You're all right. I was losing the stomach for it anyway. Stick the kettle on.' Darren indicates the kettle behind Peter. He is tired and had been looking forward to a quiet evening alone.

'I'd something better in mind than tea.' Peter pulls a glass lemonade bottle from his pocket and presents it like a sommelier. The label is washed off and it is filled with clear liquid.

'Ah,' Darren winces, 'I hardly touch the stuff anymore.'

'True, but your trips down the country often take it out of you so I thought tonight might be the night for it.' Peter's tone is soothing.

'Rinse out a pair of mugs then,' Darren says after a moment's hesitation. He sits in the worn armchair at the head of the kitchen table, anticipating the release the alcohol will bring. Peter takes two mugs from hooks above the sink, runs cold water over them and pours two generous measures.

The poteen burns Darren's throat and kindles a little fire in his empty stomach. He wants to build the fire, stack it high until it burns asunder.

'It's good stuff, all right,' Darren says, and extends the empty mug across the table.

'It's hard to believe it's made by a man who never touched a drop his entire life.' Peter uncorks the bottle, quarter-fills the proffered mug and tips a drop into the mug before him. 'You know he tests it by throwing a spoonful of it onto the fire? He can judge by the flame.'

'I do indeed. It isn't the first bottle of Mikey's hooch I've had.' Darren sips and stares into the mug. 'Well, did he tell you what kind of flame this stuff had?'

'Oh, pure fucking blue,' Peter says, aping Mikey's enthusiasm.

The two men laugh and they both take a drink.

TAWSEEF KHAN

Tawseef Khan is the 2019 recipient of the Seth Donaldson Memorial Bursary. He completed a PhD in Refugee Law in 2016 and received a Northern Writers' Award in 2017. In March 2021, he published his first non-fiction book, *The Muslim Problem: Why We're Wrong About Islam and Why It Matters* with Atlantic Books.

@itsmetawseef
tawseef.y.khan@googlemail.com

Leave To Remain
An extract from a novel

'Help me, Mrs Shah!'

I lay in bed with my eyes half closed, phone pressed to my ear, consciousness tangled up in my dreams. I was stumbling through school corridors again, on leaden legs, unable to find my classroom.

'Please help me. I don't know what to do. They take my husband and I don't know what to do.' On the end of the line, the woman began sobbing.

'Shhh, it's OK.' I sat up and pushed my hair from my face. The world was blurry. Morning fought against the pale olive curtains. 'Tell me from the top. What happened? *Who* took your husband?' I listened as the wintry November air pimpled my skin. Grabbing my glasses from the nightstand, I slipped an arm under the duvet and stared up at the clock.

For God's sake. It wasn't even 9 a.m. I had planned for a lie-in.

'The-the Home Office. One hour ago, they knock on our door and force their way in. Immigration Enforcement. My children were screaming, my husband trying to tell them we have application, but they don't care. They grab and hurt him. They force him into car and take him away.'

I heard children wailing in the background. Children who had witnessed as many as ten men dressed in black enter their home and overpower their father, shouldering him through the house and into a blue van parked out on the street. I had heard this soundtrack before, at least four times in the past three months. Immigration raids at dawn. Clients preyed on when least suspecting. Desperate, pleading calls when the sun had barely risen. I picked the sleep out of my eyes. How many more times before the year was out?

'Did they say why they were taking him?'

'No.'

'Did they give you any papers?'

'Please help me, Mrs Shah. I'm going crazy.'

I had stopped telling people I wasn't a Mrs. It didn't matter that I was only twenty-nine years old, didn't wear any rings on my fingers, and confirmed my unmarried status to anyone who asked. Most clients persisted, insisting that it was a mark of respect, and with time I resigned myself to wearing a title and an authority that wasn't completely mine to bear.

'What's your husband's name again?'

'Kulasingam. John Kulasingam. I am Mrs Kulasingam.'

'Kulasingam, OK. I'll head into the office and see what's happening. I'll try and get him out.'

'But when?'

The eternal question. The one I had no clear answer to.

'Tomorrow, hopefully? If not tomorrow, then a day or two?'

'But Mrs Shah, I need him here. He helps with the children.'

Faint details came to me through the fog of broken sleep. They had a sickly child; a learning disability, perhaps, and Mr Kulasingam was responsible for taking care of her. We had applied for leave to remain and this application was based on their life here in Britain.

'I'll try to make it as quick as I can, Mrs Kulasingam... I promise.'

I would have to get up soon. However, the last months had taught me something: it would take a while before detention officials had processed Mr Kulasingam. I still had a couple of hours if I wanted them. Another week of staying late at the office, bringing files home and working as I pretended to watch television. My eyes were sore and craving sleep. But I got up – the family's voices compelled me. I showered quickly and dressed. Within half an hour, I was ready to leave the house, grabbing a banana on the way out.

The cold outside shocked my body. I saw my breath in the air, white against the white sky, against the black branches and charred trunks. I wanted to turn back, pulled to the house by thoughts of a different day: a lazy morning in bed with breakfast followed by meeting Samir in town for coffee, the evening spent with my parents, Jahida and the kids. I saw it flickering against the street like a home movie.

I shivered as I drove to the office, waiting for the heater to kick in, the cold of the steering wheel seeping through my leather gloves. I parked at the back, where hooded youths gathered in the evenings when daylight hours were scarce, huddled around a glowing blunt. I binned the discarded beer and vodka bottles. With the press of a button on my keyring, the shutters creaked to life. I rushed inside.

It didn't matter how many times I came in on a Sunday, I resented doing this alone. Walking through the kitchen, past the dining room and toilets, into the staff work area, I still hoped to see everybody: Dad making tea in the kitchen, Rubel typing away on his computer, Babar picking at a box of mithai, Akbar daydreaming at reception. They had no obligation to be here at the weekend, but as I switched off the alarm, it struck me how empty the office felt without them, and without the clients gossiping, the phones ringing and the fax machine beeping, the doors whooshing open and slamming shut. Rarely did I have the luxury of silence when I needed to string some legal advice together – my thoughts being interrupted constantly. Still, I couldn't get used to the emptiness. I was in a fire station without my fellow firefighters – not that a fire station would ever sit on a roundabout in Burnage, the last in a sad block of shops backing onto a massive council estate.

I switched on the heating and the radiators tinkled to life. Once again, I searched for the client's file and took it into my office, ready to secure their release.

Mrs Kulasingam called the moment I sat down: 'Mrs Shah, what's happening? I'm scared.'

'Look, I'm in the office now. Let me get on,' I said. I softened my tone. 'But if Mr Kulasingam calls, tell him to contact me straight away, yeah?'

I remembered John, Mrs Kulasingam's husband. He was bearded and bald, slow moving but he caught onto my explanations of the legal process quicker than his moodier, mouthier wife. I had to get him out as soon as I could, but I wasn't optimistic about getting through, not at the weekend. I called the local Home Office department anyway. Of course, they weren't there, all I got was a dry voicemail, telling me to call back during office hours. As if they only detained migrants and asylum seekers during office hours. I tried the detainee casework team in Liverpool. I called the detention centres where he could have been taken: Pennine House and Morton Hall and Campsfield and Colnbrook, even Harmondsworth near Heathrow Airport. Each of the numbers rang out or ended with curt voice messages with the same basic information, but no guidance on what I was to do in the event of emergency. I could only sit back and wait for John to call. Once he reached the detention centre, once the detention officers had taken away his smartphone and replaced it with a pre-historic handset without any internet, once he had been assigned a room and a roommate, he would call.

I read through his file again, beginning at the end and moving forward in time. I familiarised myself with the facts I needed to build a case for his release. I knew he'd been tortured by the Sri Lankan authorities before coming to Britain – *knew* this, which should have been enough to exempt him from detention, but I had to check the reports again. The Home Office had me doubting myself.

Certain words and phrases in his medico-legal report stuck out to me: 'detained by the authorities... kicked and burned and asphyxiated'; '... twenty-eight scars, twenty-four of which were found by the clinician to be evidence of torture'; '... depression and post-traumatic stress disorder directly related to his experience of torture...'

The precise, medical terminology I could disassociate from, divorcing words from their fullest meaning, but as I flicked through the pages, I caught the outline of a human figure, a drawing that doubled up as a map of John's body, charting the scars dispersed across his stomach, back and legs. I looked away.

John rang at around noon. 'Mrs Shah, it's me. They bring me to the detention centre near Manchester Airport. I know they're going to remove me. Help me. I have a pregnant wife and three children. I can't leave. They need me.'

So he was close by, in Pennine House. 'Have they given you any paperwork?'

'They said I'm an illegal immigrant. I told them I have application, it's pending, but they didn't listen.'

'Fax me the papers from the library and I'll get to work.'

'Do something for me, Mrs Shah. They were so rough, they hurt me.'

Those three words worked their way through me. They had hurt him. What could I do about that? Who would listen to me if I tried calling attention to this? The fax machine sounded like it was in pain too, spluttering as it expelled hot air and, eventually, paper.

As decisions to detain went, the papers were unremarkable. No specificity, no originality whatsoever. John had stayed in the UK beyond the terms of his original visa. The authorities believed he was at risk of disappearing; detention prevented that. Of course, I disagreed with their assessment – he was no risk – but the fact that John had been sent to the detention centre, Pennine House, told me everything I needed to know. Pennine House was for short stays. The Home Office had taken him to the airport to stick him on a flight home.

I reached into my drawer and took out my phonebook. I had fifteen numbers for the airport, seven crossed out, as they no longer worked. One by one, I dialled the remaining numbers. I got through on the fifth attempt.

'Can I speak to the caseworker on this file?'

'Nobody's available until Monday. You can call then?'

'No, I can't. My client, Mr Kulasingam has an outstanding application.' I balanced his file on my lap. The papers weighed a ton – a whole decade of his life in this country. 'We submitted it over three months ago. We're expecting it to be accepted because his eldest child has spent seven years in Britain, and his youngest has a severe learning disability.'

Seven years was a benchmark for children; seven years in this country, speaking the language and picking up our accents and going to school and making friends; eating our terrible food and watching cartoons of pigs and trains on television. It wouldn't be right for them to start over elsewhere.

'I see,' said the officer. 'We don't have that in our records. Would you please fax a copy of the application to us?'

'Sure, but the Home Office *does* have this application, you know. I've got the acknowledgement letter here. Don't your departments liaise with one another?'

The least they could do was liaise with one another. It would mean wasting a little less of my time.

LILLIE LAINOFF

Lillie Lainoff is a writer and fencer from Washington DC. She's a graduate of Yale University, the founder of Disabled Kidlit Writers, and the 2019 winner of the LA Review Literary Award for Short Fiction. Her debut YA novel (*One For All*) is forthcoming from FSG in March 2022.

lillie@lillielainoff.com

The Mustard Children
An excerpt from a novel

When Annie walked into the half-empty bar, Tina bounded off her stool. 'You're here!' Her elbow met a cocktail glass which crashed to the bar top. Tina gasped out an apology to Annie; behind Tina, a bartender cleared up the mess of orange and shimmery drops. 'I'm so clumsy! It's a miracle I can put one foot in front of the other!'

Annie nearly turned around right then and there because there was very little she hated more than behavior like this (the purposeful self-effacement, not the clumsiness, of course – after the tumor was excised Annie had her good share of collisions with door frames and difficulty with tying shoelaces), but she swallowed the acidic reply and with a sugary smile sat on the stool Tina had saved for her. 'What are we drinking?'

Tina blinked as if she hadn't expected the question. 'Oh. Well, I had a tequila sunrise! It's silly, really. It reminds me of undergrad when I'd sneak back orange juice from the dining hall to use as mixer. We had this one vase we stored in the common room's mini fridge, and each meal I'd take one paper cup of orange juice, only one, see, so no one would catch on, and then I'd bring it back and pour it into the vase and voila! Come party time we had all the mixer we needed. Sometimes the dining hall was out of orange juice and I had to settle for apple or even Coca-Cola, which wasn't ideal, but I mean, we were kids so it's not like we cared!'

Annie had drunk once as a teenager. At a party for Homecoming, she couldn't remember who'd thrown it, but she did remember Naomi, the girl who'd held Annie's hair back while she vomited. Naomi hadn't managed to grip all the strands so some chunks had lodged in Annie's front tresses, but it was the thought that counted, wasn't it?

Tina said something else about undergrad as the bartender finished wiping down the bar top. Annie responded, although in the moment, she wasn't exactly sure what she said.

Annie's mother had been so frantic that night. She thought Annie's staggering, her vomit-rimmed mouth, her crusty eyes, that these were all signs of the resurgence, yet again, of the leukemia – regardless of how these were nothing like her symptoms. It'd been six months since Annie had last thrown up, not into a porcelain basin but into a hospital bucket. Her mother was wrong that beer-stained night. But right to worry: another round of chemo was around the corner. College applications filled out with hospital-branded pencils and pens; Annie wondered how many eyelashes and strands of hair made their way into the envelopes. Well, the admissions committees had wanted pieces of her, hadn't they; they wanted her to ladle her soul into a perfect five paragraph frame, so that's what they got: the ugly rawness of cancer, none of the romantic shit, none of the star-crossed lovers unable to kiss without risking their own immune systems – instead, Annie's lost DNA.

No more alcohol passed Annie's lips until the night she turned twenty-one. And, even then, it was just a sip of champagne. She hadn't wanted to give the tumor any reason to return. The bargaining stage: what a time.

But she was in her thirties now. She had a child. She had a husband. And she needed a drink.

Tina had been prattling on while Annie was lost in thought. Annie surprisingly felt a little bad about it – no one from the office reached out to her much anymore. (They had, of course, replied with smiling emojis to Facebook posts of her burgeoning belly and had oohed and ahhed in the comments of pictures of snoozing newborn Kerry. This was hour five, after he'd been wiped clean of blood and placenta and cried himself into an exhausted, forced sleep. But after too many sleepless nights, after 3 a.m. diaper-duty and rinsing Kerry's puke out of her favorite cable-knit sweater, Annie hardly had enough energy to fall into bed, let alone post photos. And so the comments stopped coming). But Tina, the youngest and most recent hire, only a few years out of grad school ('Washington is so much less claustrophobic than New York City, don't you think?') had been persistent to the point where Annie was forced to consider the possibility that the poor thing was friendless, hopeless, in love with her, or wanted to wear her skin like a coat.

'... I almost dropped my phone when I got your text – I was surprised! But, a good surprised, obviously!' Tina added, worry creasing her yet uncreased eyes. 'We have so much to catch up on! What do you want?'

'Hmm?'

'To drink?'

Tina flagged down the bartender as she fished for her credit card. 'I'd like another, please, and my friend will have – oh no, no, put that away,' she scolded as Annie reached for her wallet.

'Oh, I couldn't accept.'

'I insist. My treat.'

Annie wouldn't smile, didn't smile. But it was refreshing. Earnestness, so rare in this city. 'Make that two tequila sunrises.'

Tina clapped her hands. Annie's head thumped.

Two hours and one drink later, Annie's migraine had dulled to a steady murmur. It was late. She hadn't texted David. He hadn't texted her. She got lost on the way home; her mind went somewhat soupy when she drank, as if the liquor shot from her throat up her nose and rested in the tumorless cavity. She could've pulled over to search navigation on her phone, but when she tried, everything – the car, her body – it all resisted. She just had to keep on driving.

Annie's feet on the short flight of stairs to their house sounded like a broken drum, the creak of her keys against dry-skinned fingers slippery from sweat that she would've liked to have blamed on the weather if it were warm enough.

David had fought for this house, had fought hard: breakfasts in bed, foot rubs, the baptism of the apartment's kitchen counter, the apartment's bathroom counter, the apartment's other bathroom counter, all the many, many apartment counters. And when Kerry's heartbeat pulsed on the screen, such a fast and fragile thing, it was hard to protest that no, their downtown apartment was actually the perfect place to raise a child. Living things needed grass, fresh air, space to roam, room to breathe.

She'd never wanted to live in a house again. But David said that families needed houses, and that's what they were, what they were going to be, wasn't it? A family. A strange word, that, thrown around like an excuse, a curse, a prayer – did it really mean anything at all?

Annie had given David so much, and yet, he couldn't – no, he was struggling – to look past this thing – things – however small, a blip on her memory radar that she'd rather have wiped. There were very few bright sides to trauma, but wasn't one of them that it was hers, only hers, a secret deep place of her that she wasn't required to share with anyone else?

Required. Another strange word.

The door: crisp white, freshly painted once a year. Windowless, because windowed doors were asking for trouble. The threshold: caliginous, strains of dust that Annie missed while cleaning before the cleaner arrived who then missed them, too. The empty hallway leading to the kitchen, a beating pulse, a light spilling onto the floor.

'Where's Kerry?'

David swiveled toward her, body obscured by the fridge door, half of a string cheese in one hand, the other half ballooning his cheeks.

Annie snorted. 'Trying to hide that you're eating junk food?'

'Cheese isn't junk food. It has calcium and protein and—'

'—all the parts of a nutritious night-time snack. Really, you're eating something healthy for the good of the family,' Annie finished as she stepped into the outer rim of the light. She hesitated. 'Is there any left?'

David closed the fridge door. 'No, sorry, it's all gone. I'll make a supermarket run tomorrow.'

'I can do it, if you want.'

'No, no, that's fine.'

This. This was why she hadn't wanted to tell him: now – now he thought she was weak. He'd seen Kerry emerge from her, bloodied, screaming, and he still thought she was weak.

He hadn't even asked her why she was home late, where she'd been the past four hours since her appointment ended. He did care; she knew he cared; it was that he cared too much to ask. He wouldn't be afraid of the answer (an affair! how not scandalous in the city of scandals!) but he didn't want to upset her, even now.

'I'm not any different. I'm the same Annie.' Her words sounded like a plea, and she didn't like that.

David scanned the length of her: ironed white linen trousers, pale pink blouse with a collar that hung loose and supple, the dainty golden chain around her neck that housed a pupil-sized diamond.

'Both of us are different. We're old now, remember?' he said.

'Ha.'

The room was dim without the fridge door open but Annie was frozen, unable to reach for the switch. It was easier, in the dark.

'Did you ask about me attending an appointment with you? A couple's session? I did more research on the practice's website and she does have a good deal of experience.'

David's question broke Annie's thoughts, and she blinked at him. That's right. He'd asked her to look into the possibility. 'She said it wasn't appropriate. She needs more time with just me, first.'

'Huh. Well, I'd imagine you're an interesting case.'

'What's that supposed to mean?'

At the same time, he was continuing over her, voice drowning her out, 'I'm sorry, I shouldn't have said that.'

'I'm not a case,' Annie said.

'You're not a case,' David said.

'I'm a person,' Annie said.

'You're a person,' David said.

'I know things are still shitty, I'm not discounting that, but can you please just hug me? Then you can go back to being angry with me, I—'

David's arms were already around her, one spanning her shoulder blades, the other her waist. She breathed in the scent of their detergent: fresh in the way you couldn't tell what the scent was, but only that it was something unnatural, a good unnatural, the antithesis of dirt and germs and baby puke.

When she tilted her head so her cheek brushed against his scruff, her lips tracking their way northeast, he stiffened, and took a step back. His hands shifted to grip where her shoulders met her arms. And he smiled, but it wasn't a smile.

'Goodnight, Annie.'

She stood in the kitchen, fridge door suddenly popped ajar and the fans whirring and the light butter yellow on the tile, the only thing cutting through the dark, until Kerry's baby monitor illuminated with a tired, squeaking cry.

Her phone buzzed. Aiden. Another text. *Please think about it.* The photo attachment: a hole flagged with yellow marks, warning signs, a siren. *Please. Just think about it.*

MICHELE LIM

Michele Lim is a speculative fiction writer from Singapore. Her work centres on the interplay between text, narrative, and worldbuilding: she writes digital interactive fiction and is currently working on a novel-in-fragments about hallucinatory musical instruments.

@flammabir
michlim.limin@gmail.com

Wandering Point
('And all the men and women merely players')
A short story

1.

You recognise the smell of leaves and dirt. It seems you have been walking for a long time. Your legs ache. You look around, hoping someone would pick you up, but Mom and Dad are not here. You imagine them hooking their hands under your arms, lifting you, but then you realise that you don't have arms. You have four legs instead. They are thin and stiff as stilts.

Of course: you're a deer. You look around and see trees, bushes, tousled soil covered in moss. You think that maybe Mom and Dad are hiding behind the next tree, or inside that fallen log covered with speckled mushrooms. Like the peekaboo game they play with you before bedtime. So you stumble through the dirt, enjoying the cool touch of mist on your fur, on the soft flesh of your nose. You wander after a butter-coloured butterfly. You stop to chew on a flower; it tastes like strawberries, exactly as you thought it would.

You stop exploring when you realise that it's getting dark. And there's a strange new smell in the air. It tickles your nose, not in a funny way, but in a bad way. You sneeze, but the smell pushes its way even deeper into your nose. You cough, cough, cough. Maybe Mom and Dad are mad at you for yelling when they switched off the TV. You don't know where they are. You don't know why they haven't come for you.

The bad smell is getting closer. Something far away dances at you, red and orange moving quick and sneaky behind blackening trees. You start to cry.

2.

You recognise the smell of leaves and dirt. Above you, swathes of green criss-cross each other like layers of coloured cellophane. They remind you of the cardboard telescopes you made in science class this afternoon; how you put two different colours up to your eyes, red on one side and green on the other, and imagined you were on an expedition to somewhere wonderful. The trees in this place sweep high above you, like you're Jack and these are your Giant Beanstalks. As you move, you feel a gentle suction on your back, under your belly. Your eyes swivel, elongated; telescopes.

Of course: you're a snail. This forest is your natural habitat. You wonder why you are here as a snail, and why this place feels so familiar. The waves of loose sand beneath you make a pleasing rhythm, but gravity weighs down on you and your shell, a heaviness. A misgiving. You don't want to be here, you don't want to go back to school, or wherever this place is. Something bad is going to happen.

You realise that you've been in this dream before. You're not a snail, you're a person. And you know what's going to happen next. This forest is going to catch fire.

Relief washes over you. You know what you're supposed to do. You're supposed to escape. You set forward with purpose, straining, sweating rivulets of slime. But it slowly sinks in that you are a snail and can only go so far. The air trembles with heat. Trees snap and topple like dominoes.

As the canopy above you falls sideways and crashes to the ground, you finally catch a glimpse of the sky beyond the forest: a star-streaked, infinite indigo, with a pink, full moon in its centre. You stare, awestruck. It is the last thing you see.

You stay in the forest: proceed to Section 3 and 4.
You chase the moon: proceed to Section 5.

3.

It's been a while. You almost forgot about this dream, even started to think that you might never have it again. Have these trees always curved this way, their tips like fingers grazing? The longer you look, the more the boughs blur and shift, morphing: now they are church arches; now, the knitted brows of someone you love; and now, the top of a bell jar, closed over you.

This time you are a bird. Some kind of starling, by the look of your oily, tawny feathers. You preen, self-conscious, although you know that in this forest, you are always alone. You shuffle, hop, spring from ground to tree, relishing the sharp vitality in your claws, your beak.

While your dream-body scratches the dirt for worms, a part of you recognises the same heaviness that settles in your gut, always midway through this dream. You wonder if this heaviness is what summons the fire that always comes, that somehow, you're responsible for what comes next. Or if this is a primal instinct telling you to flee, even if you know you may never escape.

Still, you pump your wings. You launch yourself upward, like a missile. You anticipate resistance, tangles of leaf and bark thickening to trap you, but you only feel the rush of cool, dry air.

Open your eyes, you think – but they are already open. You are surrounded by ink, the indigo sky. Dusk stretches as far as the eye can see, flecked with silver. The moon, blushing pink, faces you like an old friend.

Beneath you, the fire rages. But you are too high up to feel a thing.

4.

You've been thinking: maybe, getting the hang of this just takes time. Now that you're back in this dream again, you slip into it as if it were a well-worn coat. You arch your back, enjoying the stretch, power rippling across your flanks. You decide to set out further than before, confident in your territory, prowling through dense undergrowth and leaping up trees, searching for the forest limits.

There must be a way out of the fire, you think; or even, a way to fight it. You wish it were here right now, in some form that you can pin and destroy with your paws. As a leopard, this is the strongest you have ever been. You find a slow stream, pausing to admire your reflection, wondering if the people who know you in waking life would stare in awe or run away in horror, if they knew that all along, there was a leopard inside of you. But they must know, if your professional success is anything to go by. Perhaps this is why you've been so lonely.

There comes that heaviness again, which has also started visiting you in waking life. You've tried dousing it with drink, but always it comes back. You start running through the forest, loping over brambles and small ponds, your body swift and fluid. It seems you have been running forever, your limbs feel as if they are on fire.

You wish you had time to climb up, to see the sky, and that moon, just one more time.

If you have been chasing the moon, proceed to your last stop, Section 3. Otherwise, keep going down to Section 5.

5.

You wonder if there is any meaning to the kind of animal you become in this dream. Other people tell you that they have recurring dreams of falling from great heights or of their teeth falling out. But you never tell anyone about the burning forest or how many years ago, as a snail, you caught a glimpse of the starry space above the trees. It sounds ludicrous when you speak it out loud. When you were younger, you went to bed wondering if you would dream this dream again, a shiver of horror and delight passing along your spine.

But those days are over. Your mind is cloudy now, weighted down by some disappointment or resentment; rollover from your waking life, you think, but you can't remember what about. All you know is that you are pushing forward, kicking and kicking against a current, but only doing enough to stay in place. 'That's life,' says a reedy, conceited voice. You aren't sure if this is something you once said, or something someone else said to you, but you toss your head sideways in annoyance. What a trite, teenage thing to say; and yet it's stuck inside of you, like a hook in your throat.

So you are a fish in a stream. Here, the sky and the trees are nowhere in sight. You only see soft, emerald weeds, circling eddies of sand. Light travels in diffused waves. You have thick, fleshy whiskers – they taste the force of water moving against you, pulling you one way, pushing you the other. But your fins and tail know what to do. They fan and sway in gentle arcs, your round, fair belly inflating with air.

If the fire is burning out there, you cannot tell. For once, you are content to forget the moon. It's hard enough work trying to forge your own path. Best to do as you've been told – to go with the flow, as they say.

Proceed to Section 6.

6.

Dread, and boredom. You drag your body against moist earth, willing the fire to come so you can wake up already. You sigh; your tongue flicks away from your face as a whistling sound comes out. Because in this form you are once again close to the ground, you catch the familiar smell of leaves and dirt – the rich, blooming scent of things growing beneath the surface. The anticipation of passing time.

But you feel tired, old in your bones. With one last, shuddering effort, you stop moving. Your skin splits, coming off you like rolling pantyhose, revealing nakedness beneath. You did not imagine that you would see this forest again after that last dream; the one where you were a fish and had given up trying to find a way out. You would sink instead, accepting gravity. The natural way forward is down.

Your eyes turn milky blind as the last of your old skin peels away.

If you have been chasing the moon, proceed back up, to Section 4.
Otherwise, proceed to your last stop, Section 7.

7.

It is dark, dark, dark. You wonder why nobody has come for you yet, why you have been left waiting. Maybe Mom and Dad are still mad at you; but they won't always be, you think. And if you stay here in the dark, they can't find you.

You suck on the sand around you, it melts through your body like sugar. You imagine that it is sweet, but really you can't taste a thing. You wriggle around, up and down, or down and up, you can't tell. This reminds you of a dream you once had that kept playing over and over, start to end, but because you always knew the ending it wasn't much fun. There was something about a strawberry moon, and fire, and running. Always running.

Maybe you were playing a game. And this is a game too – hide and seek, with Mom and Dad. That's why they haven't come for you. They're looking for you and you are hiding. This is the spot you've chosen after lots of thinking. It's cool and quiet here, down in the earth. You like it. They will never find you.

You win.

OLIVIA LOWDEN

Olivia Lowden was born in 1997 and is from Cornwall, England. She writes short fiction concerned with the underlying psychology of her characters and the nature of their relationships, focusing on themes of isolation, belonging, and desire. Her work has appeared online in several literary magazines.

lowdenolivia@gmail.com

Salvation Army
A short story

On the way to the Salvation Army, they pause on the side of a busy road. Emmeline has said something hurtful to Harry and now he is looking at her, squinting in the wind, his mouth a softly drawn line. Instead of arguing with her, he simply walks back home. He is well-versed in Emmeline's behaviour. In fact, he has put up with it for many years. He has learnt, slowly, the right moment to leave.

Emmeline stands motionless for a few seconds too long, staring at the back of his head, his receding figure. Then she turns around and carries on. The sky is a vast grey carpet above her, and she maintains a quick pace. The noise of the cars bleeds loud into her ear. So loud, it occurs to her that she shouted. When she said those things to Harry, she shouted at him.

Now she whispers. *whydidisaythat.*

A hurried and quiet confession. Words like hot metal in her mouth.

—

At the Salvation Army, a man at the desk ticks her name off a list. He hands her a small cup of orange squash and some chocolate biscuits on a napkin. For you, he says.

The lobby is poorly lit and quiet. Behind the man's head is a sheet of paper tacked to a pinboard promising a warm and friendly welcome. Emmeline hovers for a few moments, uncertain.

There, he says, and nods briefly to a door behind her.

In the waiting area, Emmeline takes a seat on a plastic chair. People are dispersed around the room, mostly alone. She starts on the squash and, despite being lactose intolerant, the biscuits. She doesn't know exactly what the Salvation Army is. She has heard the line about it in the Leonard Cohen song, but not much else. She always supposed it was something charitable yet holy, but this building stands red-bricked and monstrous on the side of a busy roundabout. Sitting inside it, she doesn't feel particularly inspired towards philanthropy or faith. She feels a little scared.

Some time passes. Emmeline is called to another room.

Right-handed? a nurse asks, taking her wrist.

Right I am, she says.

The nurse jabs a needle into her fingertip so that Emmeline winces.

The nurse looks at her but doesn't speak. Emmeline has her haemoglobin levels taken. She watches as a drop of her blood falls into a solution. It hovers for a few moments then sinks.

You're good to go, the nurse says.

Emmeline is shown to a dentist's chair and is brought more orange squash and biscuits. Shadowlike figures hurry in her periphery. On a table beside her is a small machine, some tubing. Looking at it causes a cool sweat to rise on her forehead. She has never given blood before. Harry was supposed to be giving blood too. It was his idea, actually, but they both snorted cocaine at the weekend, and Harry felt he shouldn't donate tainted fluids. He was insistent on this but offered to accompany Emmeline anyway. There was some sighing, some eye-rolling, while they had this conversation.

The nurse returns and takes her arm.

Are you OK with needles? he asks.

Kind of, she says, as he slides it beneath her skin.

He tells her to flex her hand. She obeys and feels a small pain shoot up her arm and settle somewhere in her chest.

You'll want to do that often, he says. During the process.

Emmeline settles back in the chair. Above her, the lights are painfully bright, and when she closes her eyes she sees red shapes burn like the scores of a branding iron. She continues clenching her fist, in and out. Then she thinks about Harry on Saturday night. She watched him at the party as though from a faraway place as he reclined on to low sofas with their friends, talking easily or else staring into a quiet spot, a steady and distant look across his face. Every so often he padded across the room on the balls of his feet, to snort coke or urinate. When inebriated, Harry's gait becomes soft, more so than usual. His shoulders arch high, as though being pulled upwards to heaven by invisible strings. That night Emmeline felt, as she often does, like she was viewing Harry through a glass pane. He looked delicate and untouchable, like an artefact you might find in a museum. She did not speak to him the entire night.

Emmeline tries to stop thinking about Saturday. She opens her eyes and sees the blood drain out of her in a long, snaking line. She clenches her fist and thinks that by now Harry will be back at the flat. Probably smoking a joint. It has become a habit of his, a way of removing himself from the volatility as it unfolds. He did it just last week in fact. It was evening, and they were sitting in the living room on separate sofas, a distance which to Emmeline felt huge. Harry was on his laptop, playing video games online. His face was lit palely by the screen, his eyebrows knitted together in concentration. Emmeline sat in silence, slowly thumbing the length of her index finger. Occasionally, Harry would shout and make her jump.

They're not even your friends, she said in a moment of quiet. They're my friends dressed up as your friends. If we broke up, they'd be my friends.

The words escaped her mouth like heavy, foul-smelling smoke. Her heart rate quickened. She didn't particularly mean what she said but wanted to say something.

Harry looked at her. He shook his head and slammed his laptop shut, then went outside to smoke a joint. Alone, Emmeline started to cry, although she didn't quite know what for. When she says hurtful things to Harry, she feels one stroke removed from herself, as if she is acting in a film. She spouts some poorly worded lines but ultimately, the script is something she has little control over. She thought that was something Harry knew. As she cried, she thought about the way she looked. Were her lips swelling in a flattering way? Did she look convincing? Genuine in her emotion? Candid? Did Harry think she was pathetic? Did he pity her? Did her hair look artful? Did he love her? Did she love herself?

She thought some of the answers to be yes. She thought she made a terrible actress and would likely get poor ratings in Hollywood. A director would take a chance on her as she had a face for the screen, but she'd perform terribly, mess up all her lines and walk unnaturally across the set. From then on it would be slim pickings. She'd be cast only as the bitch, earning a paltry amount in a few amateurish pilots. Eventually, she'd give up her dreams and start auditioning for porn. In this field she'd have much more success.

When Harry returned from outside, he opened up his laptop and carried on playing, and Emmeline felt a coldness wash over her. That night, she went to bed alone. An hour or so later, she looked out the window and saw him standing out the back, smoking. She looked at the sky spilling across the landscape and felt as though she was sitting at the bottom of a dense black pool. She seemed to herself unbearably alone, more so than ever before, and couldn't work out if it was her as an individual or them as a pair that was causing the pain.

She can feel the sharpness of the lights in the Salvation Army. Emmeline opens her eyes and a hot wave passes through her. She catches a passing nurse who tells her she has two minutes left.

Do you want me to remove it now? she asks.

Please, Emmeline says.

The nurse slides the needle from under Emmeline's skin. Sweat gathers on her forehead and a pain flashes behind her eyes.

The nurse looks concerned and pulls a lever that swings the chair into a horizontal position. Emmeline's legs are thrust in the air. The position makes her feel vulnerable and she visualises how ridiculous she must look.

The nurse sighs, and Emmeline once again feels like a child play-acting as an adult. The nurse asks her what she has eaten today and then laughs loudly when Emmeline says noodles. The nurse asks if she has exercised. Emmeline thinks of the forty-minute walk here and nods.

You should never exercise! the nurse says, and Emmeline nods again, because it all sounds very reasonable.

The nurse returns Emmeline's chair to the normal position and stares at her with narrow eyes.

Dizzy? the nurse asks.

Yeah, a bit.

Back down you go then.

It goes on like this for a while. Emmeline worries that maybe she isn't dizzy at all and is overthinking it. But the nurse tells her she must be fully ready to get up, that it is paramount she should not fall.

In the lobby, Emmeline calls a taxi to pick her up. The man at the desk gestures for her to take more squash and biscuits. As she waits for the car she chews slowly, the crumbs congealing in her mouth and forming a paste. She has to use her tongue to remove the sludge from her gums, sludge that even the squash cannot shift. When she exits the building, she notices the darkening sky but feels strangely light, like she has stepped off a trampoline on to solid ground.

—

Emmeline opens the front door to the flat. The hallway is damp and narrow, and Emmeline is faintly comforted by the sour smell. She takes off her coat and hangs it on a vacant hook, removes her shoes.

When she opens the living room door, she sees Harry on the sofa with his eyes shut. The only light is a waning blue coming from a small window in the corner. Fine weed and tobacco are scattered across the coffee table.

Hi, she says.

Harry is motionless and does not open his eyes when she speaks.

I'm sorry about earlier, she says, taking a step towards him. Her voice sounds strangely remote, as if it is coming from the inside of a sealed box.

I was sick, she says, moving forward again. I almost fainted at the Salvation Army, but I'm better now.

He opens his eyes and lets out a small breath. Still he does not look at her. The half-light illuminates one side of his face. His eyes look red and damp.

I'll make tea, she says.

She makes her way through to the small kitchen, boils the kettle and places a teabag in Harry's mug. She fumbles when pouring the water and spills scalding liquid on her fingers. A few minutes later, she carries the steaming drink back through to the living room with shaking hands.

For you, she says. She crouches and places the mug on the floor.

Harry finally looks down at Emmeline. His eyes are blank and glassy like impenetrable orbs. She feels afraid and curls up in a ball at his feet.

I love you, she whispers. I'm sorry.

She watches as steam from the mug rises in obscure patterns in front of her face. They stay like this for a long time, the darkness outside seeping through the small window and cloaking them.

MAX LURY

Max Lury is a British writer. He graduated from Edinburgh with an MA in Philosophy, before starting the MA programme at UEA. His novel-in-progress, *No Ghosts,* follows two unsettled people as they attempt to fill the empty spaces left when spiritual leaders and mediums declare there are no more ghosts.

maxtcl@outlook.com

The Dutchman
An extract from a short story

Bug Out vs The Steel Punishment III
Marshall Arena, Milton Keynes

The Steel Punishment is making himself vomit into a small bucket. Next to him Anna Karenina is wrapping red tape around her wrists and testing the impact-pads on her knees. The room smells of bile, and one of the lights flickers.

Yeah, Bug Out says, no, man, no. This isn't gonna work.

He scratches the shaved skin around his nipple. Pulls the glossy spandex of his pants up a little bit. Rolls his hips as he does it.

Fred wrinkles his nose. Bug Out keeps speaking.

Look, what's your cycle looking like Fred? I mean, Jesus man, your pecs are a little uneven – which is fine, sure – but coupled with, what, the circumference on your biceps must be sixteen? That won't fly.

The Steel Punishment nods as he fastens the little buckles at the top of his prosthetic leg. Dude, he says, dude. Look. You started Dbol yet?

Fred nods. Sure, yeah. Little bit of creatine as well.

Bug Out and The Steel Punishment laugh. Man, they say, you should be eating creatine for fucking breakfast.

You know there are things to help you, Bug Out says, tricks of the trade. He's rehearsing as he speaks, shadowboxing, practising grabs and switches and taunts. He curls a bicep, points out to the imaginary crowd with his other arm and bares his teeth.

Yeah, Fred says, I've heard. I'm just—

Look man, don't overthink it. Today should be easy, right? I mean the Berlin Wall is probably the biggest Heel in the business. He'll throw something dirty, nut-shot, I'm guessing, and from then on you just pound the shit out of him. Bang bang bang.

He chains together three strikes to emphasise each *bang*: right, right, left.

Fred flinches when Bug Out punches a locker next to his head and leaves a dent. That was always his reaction: he was a quiet boy, who never liked violence.

Boudicca walks in, glistening with sweat, to a small round of applause. Thank you, thank you, she says, giving mock bows to the locker room crowd. She washes blue paint from her face in the cracked porcelain sink in the corner of the room, wiping the dirty mirror with her hand so she can see her reflection.

She nods her head towards the corridor leading to the ring. Big crowd tonight, she says, enough heat to go around. Don't worry boys, and she flashes a grin, we left them wanting more.

She pauses for dramatic effect.

Always do.

Laughter from the benches.

Bug Out runs a hand through his greasy hair which catches the light above. He's tall and his eyes are too big for his face; they bulge like there's pressure being applied behind them. Ladies, he says, what do you think about our Fred?

Who's he meant to be again? Anna Karenina moves closer, removing her silk babushka's scarf, a repurposed communist flag that's been cut into red strips.

The Flying Dutchman? She says. Wow. Big boots to fill, literally. He was your daddy, right?

Fred winces at the word. He was my dad, yeah.

But in Fred's head he was never dad, always the Dutchman. He was the man who'd wake him up when he came home after a match, still buzzing, who'd tell him with wide eyes of the men he fought with his bare hands. Who'd drink beer and call him my son and tousle his hair.

Anna Karenina nods. Sorry for your loss. She half-leans into a conversation from the other side of the room before turning back to the boys. But yeah, she says, what're you taking?

Just started Dbol.

She shakes her head. Right, she says, not going to work. You got him on FD yet?

It's Bug Out who speaks. It's only been a few weeks, Anna. Give the guy a break.

Let's not fuck around, she says. You wanna be a Face? Fine, cool. You've got to be jacked. Who's going to root for someone like that? She gestures to Fred.

Hey, The Steel Punishment says, no need for that.

She shrugs, like, don't shoot the messenger.

She pauses, looks at the limp costume on the bench next to Fred.

I mean, she says, does that even fit?

It doesn't. He tried it on yesterday. The green vest that's meant to be skin-tight sags in all the wrong places and the spandex pants are a little loose. Even the mask, fake barnacles beading at the temples, two tentacles swooping under the eyes, leaves little sores where it pinches the skin around his nose.

Fred stays mute, shifts his weight on the seat. The empty costume fills the room.

Yeah, she says. My point exactly.

Fred thinks of the funeral three weeks ago, how he had worn the suit he and the Dutchman shared – they could only afford one – and how it had hung loose from his shoulders, how the long sleeves had brushed his knuckles.

The suit had made him look like a child, he thinks, like he was playing dress-up whilst home alone.

Bug Out coughs. Hey, Fred. Thoughts?

Fred stays mute. Bug Out looks at him for a while.

You look just like him, you know that?

Fred nods. He does not think he looks much like the Dutchman at all. The man was made grotesque by Human Growth Hormone: he had bubble gut, his stomach bloated and distended like a hard boil. He thinks of the Dutchman towards the end. How pumping your body full of experimental Chinese steroids and shooting insulin pre/post-workout on top of regular doses of synthetic-HGH makes your organs swell and swell until they smother each other and burst like overripe fruit.

He remembers how he had felt sitting alone in his car outside the gym, hearing the doctor say we are so sorry but there was nothing we could do in the end, holding the phone to his ear even though the line had gone dead. He had thought he might burst too: that whatever dark thing had taken root in his body would balloon until it split his stomach right down the middle.

The Steel Punishment wipes the back of his mouth with his hand. Spits. Look man, he says to Fred, I'll be blunt. You need energy. He puts a hand down his throat again, casual, like plucking an eyelash, and heaves. You ever try this?

He takes a small paper packet from his pocket and unfolds it. He says this'll help and then some, sticking a finger – still wet with bile and spit – into the greasy powder and rubbing a smear on his gums.

Fred thinks for a moment. He looks around the room; no one gives them a second glance.

The Dutchman would always say you're too smart for this, Fred. You don't want to follow in your old man's footsteps. But Fred did. That was the problem. He wasn't as clever as the other boys and he couldn't do funny, and it broke his heart whenever his parents had praised him because he wanted to say, you're wrong, you just think that because I'm your son, I'm just scraping by in class and I have no friends and every day I eat lunch on my own in a dirty corner of the playground.

He follows suit. He wonders if the Dutchman did this too, took part in these small rituals, these private concessions. It tastes like petrol.

You got a girl, Fred? Anna Karenina asks.

Nah, he says. No time.

Oh?

Doing a degree at the same time. Paying for it by doing this. Barely even have time to—

Jack off?

No, he says, and blushes. Not that, I meant—

Sure, she says. I mean, probably impossible with all that shit in your system.

Fred's gums go numb and he feels something at his centre go cold. It still works, he says, works just fine.

Anna smirks. Sure it does, sweetie.

He reaches for more.

Hey, easy, Fred. The Steel Punishment laughs.

I'm kidding. Knock yourself out.

A voice from the corridor: on in five.

A cheer as he stands. He can tell they're trying to big him up, to make him feel like part of the family. He fist bumps a couple of people close to him, and shakes hands with the Berlin Wall, who has tied his grey hair into a long plait that hangs down to just above the faux-concrete belt he wears. Good luck, he says. Just like we practise.

Sure, Fred says, just like we practised.

The Berlin Wall says something else but it's lost in his broken English. Fred nods, and they make their way towards the corridor, and out into the ring.

It's over like that.

He doesn't join the gang for a beer afterwards. He doesn't know why; just shakes his head when they offer.

As he leaves the small building The Steel Punishment runs to catch up with him. He takes four small glass bottles from his bag, and a handful of needles, and passes them to Fred. Look, he says, go easy on the stuff. It's FD-40. They say once a week, but, hey, two or three times won't kill you. Got it?

Fred nods.

Once he's in his bedroom he gets naked in front of the mirror and stands there for a while. He takes his measurements and puts them into an online calculator called *The Greek God Physique* and realises he has a way to go: his ratios are way off. He sits on the end of his bed and takes a needle – filling it by piercing the rubber seal of one of the bottles – and slips it into his hip. The puncture is quick and leaves a little red dot of blood.

He sits for a while, until he realises he's been tapping his foot on the floor like a jackhammer. He stands up and walks a few laps of his apartment. He is filled with so much energy he puts his head in his hands and breathes and feels his whole body throb.

The cash from the last two matches is just enough to pay rent: he can keep the sofa they spent every Christmas squeezed onto, the chair his mum would read the paper on in the morning, the wonky chest of drawers the Dutchman built when she was sick.

He reps out a few bicep exercises, and starts organising the huge stack of bills the Dutchman left: some curling at the edges from the damp; some from months ago splattered with beer or coffee; handwritten notes from the dealers who would sell his father Turinabol and Enanthate-Testosterone in the disused sauna of the local gym. Sometimes he finds his mouth moving around words and realises he has been talking out loud to an empty room.

Sleep swallows him like the sea: in the dark and all at once.

Bug Out vs The Dirty Habit IV
Wolverhampton Civic Hall, Wolverhampton

He works out with Bug Out in Bug Out's garden. It's small and cramped but the walls are high so the neighbours can't look in. It's all cracked paving tiles and dirty drooping weeds and littered with empty cans. Bug Out puts his laptop on a table nearby and watches a porno whilst he does sets of curls.

There's an old Wendy house in the corner, plastic and stained brown. Fred asks if Bug Out has a kid and he just shrugs. Not anymore, he says. He looks at it a little while longer whilst Fred busies himself with crunches.

Bug Out and Fred don't say much else that afternoon. Occasionally spot each other on the bench or check form. They take breaks to take small shots of FD-40 or to drink instant coffee out of novelty mugs. Sometimes

Bug Out will comment on the video. He'll say something like, nice, real nice. Or, that's how you do it mate. Just like that.

JAMES MILDREN

James Mildren is writing an autobiographical novel called *Antagonism*. Set in London and Berlin, the novel recounts the breakdown of a romantic relationship, exploring aesthetics, memory, alienation, feminism, work-life balance, performativity, privacy, narcissism and the various connections which exist between these things.

james.mildren91@gmail.com

Easter Sunday
An extract from Antagonism, a novel-in-progress

'What time are people arriving?'

'I told them midday.'

'Maybe we should start cooking soon,' I say.

'Yeah.'

The beginning is always difficult.

I pause to remember the ingredients and steps. I am impatient to find my rhythm, to know what comes next, barely thinking, to disappear entirely in the making of something, in a trance state which hardly ever arises from chopping vegetables.

'*Pardon*,' Léa says, reaching for bowls in the cabinet above.

Celery lies on the counter. I rip off four stalks. Their sprawling florets have not been touched by some unseen industrial process. We bought them yesterday from a cart at Boxhagener Platz. The grocer weighed them, keeping tally of the price on a pocket calculator. The absence of plastic packaging and the absolute requirement to pay in cash gave the experience an authenticity not available in supermarkets. Black speckles gather on the underside. I run them under the tap. The water splashes around the steel basin, thrown by the vegetable's curved interior.

I halve the peeled onions. The knife separates spherical layers of skin. When the metal meets wood my wrist flicks to start that same motion a millimetre to the left, continuing until vertical slices bundle between clenched fingers. They rotate the shape ninety degrees and the cutting resumes. Except the surface layers, loosened by those thin incisions, no longer hold. They bend under the blunt blade, dissipating the downward force laterally. And the knife slips, bringing me back. The aim for precision complicates, with this blunt knife and nothing to sharpen it.

I dice larger chunks. The white scales multiply in a disorderly pile. I push them flatly, out of the way: rough random shapes, subject to further manipulation. The pile grows. Now there is no space on the wood. I scrape them on to a plate's blank white surface. Then I do the celery and carrots. The tricolour pile reminds me of Ireland. I shove the knife and yank around in the opened tin of tomatoes. Its insides separate against the blade. I take care not to slosh the vicinity with acidic red drips.

Léa sits, carefully measuring flour and oat milk into a bright green bowl. We often spend mornings this way, co-operating. Veganism's constraints are automatic, dissatisfaction: a phantom. The limits it imposes govern us and in so doing, vanish.

The oil is shimmering. Onions land with a hissing sizzle. I drop the knife and its cheap metal clanks the hob's black glass. With bare fingers I push stray bits into the pan and set the plate down beside me. I stir awhile.

Salt. I don't find it.

'Where's the salt?'

'I'll bring it to you.'

The box of salt is next to her on the table, for the pancake mix.

The heat requires my constant vigilance. She peers over my shoulder, her hand on my back. Her fingers grip the box daintily. The posture renders her palm concave. She leaves the box there next to me.

'It smells good,' she says.

'It's just onions.'

My arm finds her waist. She motions with her chin and I kiss her, short and decided. Impatience to cook clouds everything and my arm soon goes. Her straight arms squeeze my midriff a second longer.

'I'll start the pancakes now,' she says. 'Can I take that ring there?'

'Sure.'

I sprinkle large salt crystals over the yellowish onions. The other vegetables go in. That light sizzle stops at first. But the hob's heat overwhelms the water's cool resistance. A deeper rustle sounds among the odd orange and pale green bits. Their colours dull as water ebbs into rising steam sucked up by the extractor fan. Everything softens while I wait to add smoked paprika, cumin, dried coriander, beans and tomatoes.

'Mmm,' Léa says, holding a flat spatula upright.

The first pancake looks sad next to her. The second bubbles around submerged blueberries. She slides the spatula between the smoking pan and the cake's underside, twisting to flip the gas-filled patty, which lands and slams, sliding.

'Shall we have that first one?'

'Yeah,' she says. 'It didn't come out well.'

'The first one never does.'

She brings folded warmth to my lips. Bitter purple explodes in the mouth. The heat has eviscerated the blueberries. Fatty undercooked batter returns pastel textures.

'I see what you mean. But the rest will be OK.'

'The pan needs to get hotter,' she says.

Léa ladles more batter which spreads, sets and rises. My beans simmer. Fierce squelches sound when I coax stuck mix from the pan's edges. I switch off the hob, leaving the pan there to absorb the remaining heat.

I remember the first time cooking this for her. Her mother's birthday brunch: New Year's Eve 2018. By then it was already instinctive. An unknown recipe leaves me moving back and forth to decipher instructions. Time passes and nothing happens. Until those words become a physical meal, their mysteries unveiled – in action.

'I finished the beans,' I say. 'What else can I do?'

'Could you finish the pancakes, so I can start getting ready?'

'Sure.'

'Thank you.'

Probably two pancakes in that bowl. The settled cream batter swills into the ladle. I know the pan is too hot but I don't have the patience. I add one to Léa's stack and cook the next in a rush too. Finally, that awful extractor fan is off.

I hear inviting trickles on their way down the drain, through the half-open bathroom door. That's right: her flatmates are away. The kitchen is a mess behind me.

That shower sound becomes louder. Sporadic splatters fall all at once. The humid air reaches my skin and nostrils. The clothes irritate and chafe. The top rolls off. I peel the trousers slower, balancing on one foot and tugging the bottom cuff over each heel until denim rubs my calves.

The entrance gives no view to the room. I arrive, naked. She stands, fingers tracing through darkened hair, clumped together and wet, her eyes closed. They open. And she is nonchalant. I belong in her languid gaze. The belonging supplants all desire for her soft body. Eyes glancing down, she returns to her hair.

She half steps, shoulders opening. The area is vast, no doors. She keeps the temperature high, not liking the cold. I writhe to douse unexposed patches. Immersion takes me away from sight. My skull breaks the stream. Ticklish rivulets run over me. Open eyes show her lathered hands replacing black soap on the rack. They caress my wet skin. I lift my arms and she steps closer. The soap is soon absorbed in my armpits' wiry black hairs. The skin is blotchy and red there.

'What happened here?' she says.

'I get it from swimming.'
'Shall I put some cream on it?'
'No, it's OK.'
Then she does my back.

On my return, she moves her fingers around my balls and my penis twitches.

After rinsing I say, 'Let me do you.'
'OK, but quick,' she says.

I focus heavily on the breasts, she notices, smiling at my baseness. My right shoulder presses her collar bone to the wall, a faint force she likes. But why does the vagina roughen when water gets in? The clashing water overpowers her breath's sound and I retreat to study her face.

'People will be here soon,' – her glance completing the message.

I withdraw from her.

She rinses and leaves, taking the Moroccan towel she left bundled on the closed toilet seat. I turn the taps. Her preferred temperature has me sweating. Waiting to get cold, I decide not to wank my erection away, watching it deflate instead. Carrying a clean towel, she catches this abject scene.

'Aw, poor James,' she says.
'Sex is not such a bad reason to be late to a party, you know.'
'Not when you're the host!'

I dither, cooling. Sometimes a shower doesn't hit the spot. Quiet from shutting the taps comes abruptly. The hands scrape off water from my stomach and thighs. Isolated drips from the showerhead fall at random.

Léa is before the bathroom mirror. Her drawer is open. Inside, too many creams, bottles, tubes and tubs for the eye to separate. With her finger, she massages shiny white oil into her face. The reflection meets her eye from the mirror's surface. It shows her image, but not her. What she sees is similar, but her asymmetry is represented in opposite. Something of her hides in that sad mirror: hidden by the act of looking.

She puts the cream away and leaves. I spit minty white foam to the basin, rinse, spit again and dab my mouth's boundaries. My eyes scan the image too, familiar in that dreamy, distracted state. It's always impossible to cross that chasm, the transparent barrier which shuts away the real world. As a child in the department store, I would run past the rows of mirrors then stand behind them, confused by their flatness and the illusion of depth. If I catch myself in the mirror unexpectedly, there is a disturbing, momentary glimpse of what everyone else sees. Some people don't have mirrors in their house.

Fresh air passes through the apartment's open doors and windows. Discarded bottles jangle outside. A bin door slams closed in the courtyard downstairs, noise bouncing off tall walls. The gentle draught collects moisture from my skin.

Léa stands by the wardrobe's full-length mirror in only panties. A hairdryer begins to whir high-pitched furies. I might have approached her except the motorised shrieking is too unpleasant. Passing her, hot dry blasts reach me. Her hair lightens.

It will be warm again today. I step into shorts. The polo shirt Léa bought for my birthday has crumpled slightly in my bag. I was saving it for this. She knows what suits me. I roll deodorant on first.

That loudness stops as she snaps the switch.

'What time is it?' she asks.

'Eleven thirty.'

I drift, dressed, back to the kitchen.

ADEOLA OPEYEMI

Adeola Opeyemi is a Nigerian writer and editor. A 2020 Miles Morland Foundation scholar at UEA, her work has appeared online and in print. You can find her hiding behind this Twitter account @Adeola_Opeyemi, where she shares her unpopular opinions on books and music.

Opeyeade@gmail.com

Of Home and Other Places We Claim

Eyes – they peer at me all day. Eyes with glasses and eyes without. Eyes with bemused expressions. Eyes with cold blank stares that light a fire and burn a man's spine down. Eyes that carry questions delivered by tight-lipped men.

Who are you?

Are you marking the city for a terrorist group or a drug syndicate?

The questions won't stop coming. They come in torrents and trickles – these questions carried by men who are angry, confused or scared. They come in black suits and speculations – these men. They come in white lab coats with curiosity. I prefer the scared ones. They stay a few feet away, a barrier between us, and make promises. I can see it in their eyes; everything unfamiliar is dangerous.

The asylum is not a prison. Tell us who you are and what woman you are talking about. We will treat you and let you go, the men in white lab coats promise.

So I ask them my questions. I have been asking for months now, perhaps weeks. I am not sure how long it's been.

Where is the woman who was sitting by me when you took me?

The men in white coats say my memory is faulty. They smile when they say it. The kind of smile that says I know better than you.

There was no woman, they say. Perhaps you cannot remember much.

The medications and the questions create a fog in my brain. Everything seems like a long time ago – everything except Felicity and the woman.

It was a Wednesday or a Thursday. One of those days when you're unsure what to do with yourself; everyone walked a bit slower, smiled guardedly and held their frustration at the tip of their fingers, ready to unleash it on their cars' horns, their work emails or a waiter who served the wrong meal. Everyone except me.

I was certain of everything I would do that day. Deliberate even in my choice of clothing. I wore the grey Armani suit that Felicity bought me on our second wedding anniversary.

I stood in front of the mirror for a long time that morning, making sure my tie was right, a perfect Windsor knot – just the way Felicity taught me. I hesitated a bit while trying to pick the right pair of shoes. Felicity had made me pack the expensive ones.

They would come in handy for dinners with friends, she had said, animatedly.

I didn't have the heart to ask her what friends? What dinners? She knew no one in Nigeria, and I hadn't been home in fifteen years. I packed the shoes anyways.

I fetched a pair of taupe Church's Oxfords out of the shoe rack and put them on. They were the most expensive thing I bought in my sixth year in the UK. Six years of smiling at strangers and colleagues who asked casually in conversations if I felt lucky to be away from the wars and poverty in Africa. Six years of smiling and agreeing with them over a cup of warm tea, dry gin and cold camaraderie that I was indeed lucky to have escaped home.

The first time I saw the Church's pair, they were on display at Harrods. I'd stared at the price tag for a long time; half my salary as a specialist registrar. When a polite attendant asked if I'd like to see other designers and ushered me towards cheaper brands, I refused, sauntered back to the Church's and asked for the shoes to be packed. That month, the hunger pangs in my stomach grew into an aversion for the pair, but I didn't mind. It was my five minutes of respite against constant assumptions that being different meant being small.

As I left my apartment that morning, I ticked one thing off my mental chore list for the day.

Dress impeccably well, for Felicity. Checked ✓

There was a political debate on the radio as the cab made its way into the city. The ailing president had returned to the country under the cover of darkness. There were no pictures to prove this. A member of the opposition party was ranting about the danger of hiding the president's health issues. The military might take over the government, he warned. I hissed and asked the cabman to change the station.

Tapping my feet to Orlando Owoh's 'Kangaroo' blaring from the new station, I stared through the side window as my cab drove past Rumueme, Rumuafrikom, Rumuochita, so many *rumus* swirling into one city. I smiled at the hypocrisy of such a divided community prefixing its neighbourhoods' names with a familial identity.

The cab stopped at Rumuola. I stood rooted to a spot, the city crowd spilling everywhere without a glance at me. It was the same spot where

I had discreetly spread Felicity's ashes a week earlier. I had hoped that I could feel Felicity in the air, but there was only the smell of bole and smoked fish from street vendors.

It had always been Felicity's desire to be forever free in the city that once exiled her parents. After participating in a failed coup in 1976, her father, a colonel, had fled Nigeria with his pregnant wife. Felicity had always dreamt of seeing home. When the doctors told us Felicity's lung cancer had reached its final stage, it seemed like the last chance to return to Nigeria.

The first few weeks were hard, but as we began to face the inevitable exit, we began to talk more about her impending death and burial.

Cremation is not an African thing, Licy, I told her. No one burns a loved one's body here.

I don't want a grave, she'd argued. I don't want you attached to a piece of land.

But she had been wrong. Even without a graveside to return to, it seemed wrong to return to London without Felicity. I'd changed my flight ticket a few times before cancelling it. There was an emptiness in me so heavy it could only be worsened by leaving the city without my wife.

Come to the spot where you spread Felicity's ashes. Checked ✓

A passer-by brushed my shoulder; I was startled. I looked around, remembering where I was. I checked my watch; it was 3:32 p.m. The crowd on the street was growing bigger every minute. The sweat stains stamped on starched shirts of bulky men returning from works. The frustration stamped onto the faces of women fending off traders and touts' offensive hands. I saw them all. It was the perfect time to tick the last chore on my list.

I took a breath and moved farther into the street, ready to end it all and see my Felicity again.

That moment was the first time I heard her voice – a peal of familiar laughter rising above the madness of the city. I paused, looked across the road in the direction of the voice as a car honked at me.

I hurried across the busy road, defying nasty okada riders on their way to hell. And there she was – the woman and her strings of laughter. She sat primly on a mat made of cartons by the roadside, half laughing and half singing money out of the pockets of passers-by. I watched her in awe.

There were others seated beside her. Others who looked just like her – eyes like coffee drops in a pool of milk, feet darkened with henna and the trauma of trudging away from home, indigo chiffon wrapped around their waists and heads.

I'd seen people like her before. They were everywhere in the city, these people.

A group of them had surrounded our cab the day I arrived in Nigeria with Felicity. When I tried to shoo them away, she'd asked who they were and why they looked different from everyone else.

Tuaregs from Niger, I told her. Bombarded Nigeria after famine hit their country in 2005, now they hang around every city, harassing people for money. Vermin! I'd huffed, glaring at a young boy who thrust his dirty hand into the open side window.

I would never forget the look in Felicity's eyes that day. It was a look she'd spared me a few times in our marriage. I recoiled immediately, but I couldn't take back the words I'd said.

As I stood watching the Tuareg lady laughing at the antics of a half-naked child grabbing pedestrians' legs and lobbying money out of their pockets, I understood Felicity's silent rebuff.

It took me a while to realise what was familiar about the laughter that drew me away from the street. It was a burst of laughter I'd heard before, travelling across rooms and yards in our Dulwich home. The laughter that was eaten away, one cough at a time, as the tumour in Felicity's throat grew tentacles and took over our lives.

I stood at the same spot until she was done laughing. I watched as night sneaked upon the city, and she tucked her money into a tiny purse, bade farewell to her co-beggars and disappeared into the night. I was at the same spot long after she left, and dawn spread its canopy over Port Harcourt and beyond.

The last chore on my list remained unchecked.

I was back the next day, and the days after that, standing by the walkway, staring at this woman whose laughter pulled me away from death. There was always something new to stare at, something new to remind me of home, of Felicity.

There was her temple, folding into thin layers like expensive satin when she smiled. The slight curl of her lips when she was peeved. And when she invited me to sit with them on the fourth day, there was the faint smell of the jojoba oil in her hair, just like Felicity's. There were the uncomfortable ones, too: her fist rubbing her thighs in a way that was neither aggressive nor comforting when a stranger spat in her bowl. There was the squaring of her shoulders when an older man asked her to return to her country. There was the scoff, loud enough to latch itself on the back of its victim, when a young man had propositioned her – you better marry me, he'd said, or you will be sent back to your country and die of hunger.

I recognised it all: the disdain wrapped in pity and passed off as charity by pedestrians; the superiority in their hasty looks as they clutched their bags tighter and walked faster; everything that reminded me of my early years in London. Of the years before I learnt to square my shoulders and own the rooms I walked into. The years before I mastered the art of hiding my accent under the hard *r* and soft *t* of my phoney British accent. Of the years I learnt also, that home is wherever you make it.

It was strange how she never asked me who I was or what I wanted. She'd welcomed me with a smile every morning and made room for me on the mat as I resumed with her group, sitting in my Armani or Tom Ford suit, receiving alms and curious glances from passers-by.

Soon the pedestrians became spectators. School children with missing socks, dirty shorts and ashy knees. Adults holding tight to the content of their pockets, one eye feasting on me, the other roaming in search of pickpockets. A growing crowd amused by a beggar in designer suits. Growing until it made room for TV and radio reporters in faded crew vests and smug looks. Growing until it merged all assumptions into one phrase – a sick, rich man.

They came eventually – the government health workers. They dragged me off the mat and pulled me towards a waiting ambulance.

Let her come with me, I begged.

Who?

Her, I said, looking back at her expressionless face. She looked so much like Felicity at this point. Had she always looked like that?

They stopped midway, hands still gripping me, and told me there was no *her*. There was never anyone sitting by me.

VICTORIA OSBORN

Victoria Osborn was born and raised in Norfolk, from a multinational background. She is working on a novel about the kidnapping of a selkie on the North Norfolk coast, exploring secrets individual and generational, and people's changing relationships with the land. Victoria also writes short fiction, weaving in themes around climate change, landscape, place and displacement.

vaepenn@yahoo.com

5831. Tishrei

It is hot up on the roof.

Sometimes when the sun is at its highest we have to lie very still and feel the tiny stones from the grey fibre that covers the flat roof stick to the sweat of us, and then the silent buzz of the inside of our skulls will calm, calm down.

From up here, we can look across to other people's rooftops, to the blue house nearby where the sheet tied across poles has pink flowers on it, to the house with the ivy where they have a tent up. It must be very sticky inside that, we think.

The umbrellas we have tied to the drainpipes were once red, but like a wish have faded in the light. Fungal, they spread out from the pipes, and so the shade they cast slinks creaturely around the flat roof throughout the day. The mattress we managed to force out through the big window has a sag in the centre where a spring has given way, but we don't mind if we find ourselves curling like fiddleheads in to each other. It would only be how we were at the start of all things, together, in the womb.

When the Flood first came in it was slow and certain as a song. The sea kept coming, as everyone had been saying, and the horizon spread out, bitter-tasting; but this easterly city stood on slightly higher ground so at first everyone moved here. People filled it up like a new high tide, crammed in with friends, borrowed rooms, took over hotels; but as the salt edged closer they drained away again, by oar and pole and motor further west and north. And then the waters slid into the city, an uninvited guest, rose up along the streets, were here to stay.

But we stayed too, my sister and I, and the others, the left-behinds, in our suddenly quiet city. We didn't want to leave. We didn't know what would happen next.

Sky all around, and all around is sea. From the water, houses rise stunted in labyrinthine brick mesas. Packs of gulls bob past windows; there are no other birds. Sometimes we see fish in the water; they are spiny, the pallid brown of olive fruit, and we have agreed wordlessly that we do not want to catch them. Do not want to eat them.

When we read to each other, we speak in voices. We only have seventeen books in the cardboard box – we have counted – and we lie on our mattress, or with our heads on the rough burr of the rolled-up carpet, and live out the stories again. A few of the books have got wet and have had to be dried out in the sun; the pages have gone wavy, curved like roof tiles. We know their insides well, too well, can repeat them in chunks without looking, correct each other's mistakes. Sometimes when we finish one, we start again at the beginning.

She is halfway through a sentence when she falters. She ought to know this by the bone, and I raise myself onto my elbows to interrupt, but she sticks her foot in my face.

Is that a parakeet? she says.

A fervid green, the bird shuffles sideways, iron dark claws tapping on the guttering. We stand in long seconds until, very loud, it takes off into the blue abrasive sky.

The gulls are not the only creatures who take to the waters. In the morning, when the sun has not yet got up to full glare, we watch the Woman in the Straw Hat go off on her wooden pallet, paddle dipping like a beak. There is food in shops and houses, scattered, picked upon. We have a desk that floats; but only one will fit at a time. The Man with Three Boys has an actual rowboat, large enough for all four of them together. The Man has swapped some food with us before, thrown packets and tins up to our roof and we've dropped things back down to him. We won't get closer, though.

We have never heard the children speak.

When the city first started filling with people, the local radio station ran in a constant churn of talk: information about flood patterns, places to stay, food provision. And then like creeping damp the non-stop chatter turned a bend and became routes further inland, last dates for exodus, planned arrival cities. A hammering upon the ears. Slowly, as the floating rush streams away over the weeks, so does the urging voice, until it at last goes quiet.

Six weeks later, our wind-up radio sputters into life. There's music, after so long, song after song, and a boy, a boy somewhere out there, who talks and talks like he knows we're out here, talks until his voice becomes rough, until we can hear him swallow. And we talk back, my sister and I, we laugh and we answer him like he can hear us. This lasts a whole year. But one day the boy turns off the music in the middle of the song, and his voice is loud, and like machinery it grinds together, and then he cries.

The radio has been silent since then.

The parakeet is back. A faint breeze curls the feathers on its chest into chrysanthemum petals. My sister crumbles crackers between her palms; I snatch the box back from her while she scrapes sweaty crumbs from between her fingers onto the floor. The bird hops down, beak staccato. Its legs, close to, are parched, arid. It doesn't stay for long.

The days are full of hours. Time sits on our shoulders like the heat does. We wind up the radio just to listen to the handle turn. We sing to each other, songs that we remember, or part remember, not always the same part. We help each other out with the words. Sometimes we disagree. Sometimes we dance.

She has gone to restock, out looking for food. We hope for things in tins; boxes; exchangeables. I watched her earlier, long pole in hand, ferrying herself away on our upturned desk. I watched the light move on the dark knot of her hair until she reached the corner; then she turned, and was out of sight. It is very empty on the roof now. I pick through the mattress cover until the broken spring is visible, then flip it over so the damage is hidden. The shadows swing through the red-capped umbrellas. There's a hollow knocking, coming from below. I look over the edge of the roof. The Man with Three Boys is tapping on our drainpipe with an oar.

When my sister gets back I tell her what the Man with Three Boys said. That they were leaving, too. That it was past time to go. That space could be found, but it would have to be now. And she listened, and she said Smell these. Oranges. It's been a long time, hasn't it? Don't they smell like sunshine?

We are quarrelling more, now. We have stopped singing together, unable to agree on the words. When I read, she sits silent, the curve of her jaw turned away.

The final orange lies splayed, a bright star, between us. She takes the last piece, and I bite her. I feel the skin of her hand part, damp, delicate, under my teeth.

With an uttering of wings, the parakeet lands on the drainpipe. Each dark eye watches in turn as its neckruff twists. Something, a twig, is gripped in its bladehook beak. What's that? I say, and I stand and edge close. What's that you've got there? And it lets that twig fall, and lunges forth, quick as flame.

It bites.

And, warm as blood, the rain begins to fall.

Present Tense

What it reminds me of is a picture in a magazine seen in childhood. All in tones of gold like the dying blast of a sun: a photograph of a salamander trapped in amber. One back leg is forever outstretched, hurdling here from twenty million years ago. Within this still life, the detritus of a Caribbean creek, plant scraps floating eternal. There is, in my memory, startlingly little difference between the colour of the salamander's resin prison, and the bright warning yellow of the *National Geographic*'s covers.

At my feet, the fish could be behind old runnelled glass, a museum display. It's rare now to have a winter cold enough for this, and I stand on the ice with care. Not far below it, I can make out the dark travelling flow of water still passing down the fen dyke. From snub nose to tail a polished-leather brown; tawny dappling runs like paint spatter along belly and throat. Surely if I stand here long enough, unmoving, unbreathing, at last the fish will blink.

In past times there used to be long heavy winters, and even the great waters would ice over so thick that people could set up stalls on them, festivals of life and light and darting chaos on that dense stillness. In paintings, these Frost Fairs are a whirl of humanity in muted commotion, shades of drabs against the ice, London sedan chair or revels of Dutch clogs, silent open mouths red like organs, like livers, and to one side crows pickpicking at a fallen horse, always; always a memory of death in life.

My ears ring with the quiet. Like a last breath a frost blister balloons two feet beyond the fish. The surface is scuffed, powdery where I stand. By the clump of sedge further down a chunk of ice calves off, then disappears.

A cranking of geese in the air, and I look back over the fen. Dark lowness sifted with silver, a mackerel sky rinsed clean in bars of palest blue, and oaks scribbled black against it. Drains and drains, slicing at flat angles, stretching up to the Wash and out. My toes clench to remember the times we went skating here, as children, slipping and nonnicking along cuts and dykes. I haven't thought about that for years.

That passing gooseflight, and I see as sure as if those bodies are lofted unsteady in the air before me now, the sweated knit caps and rubber boots of dyke leapers. Thighs thresh over fen, pale flesh mudsmeared like parsnips exposed to the light, then leap – to hover at the long pole set ready in the water before coming straight down to the bank beyond, like a tree felled. Faint clapping becomes the wingwhirr of starlings, and I look to the ice at my feet.

It is grubby, as though touched by seven generations of hands. Bits of brash caught within; leaf and twig and split end of reed. The fish is there, still, slick brown back and fragile spreading fins. Black water creeping inches below. I wonder about it, frozen here, and what might happen after the thaw comes. Could it still be alive, suspended in ice time, waiting for release to slip away? Which of us will wait longer, watching?

Perhaps my fish will one day float away in his own ice fragment, unwitnessed.

The wool of my scarf itches my throat as the sun heats up.

JONATHAN PADWAY

Jonathan Padway is an American writer from Milwaukee, Wisconsin. After receiving a BA in History and Political Science from the University of Wisconsin-Madison in 2013, he spent eight years working in international diplomacy and development. His novel-in-progress, *Negatives*, explores the post-colonial bias of the international development industry through the eyes of a photographer.

Jpadway12@gmail.com

Negatives
Extract from a novel

We pulled up to the school, mud stuck in our tires and splattered over our clothes. It didn't suck us in but chunks flew with every step, sticking to our shoes and releasing with the force of freeing our feet. I kept my camera in its case.

'Now, remember,' said Ron, the guy who had traveled with me and was some sort of program manager or expert from the Firm back in Washington, DC, and who, like me, was also visiting the Country for the first time, 'it's imperative that you get photos of the kids with the books, reading them, smiling. We need to show our donors that they're not only enjoying the fruits of their donations but are also learning something from their generous charity.'

'It would be a lot easier if I could use my digital camera. That way I can at least see what I'm taking pictures of. Cost effective for you guys, too.'

'Authenticity is key. Film has a nostalgic and real quality that digital simply can't replicate. It's a cornerstone of our marketing strategy and the reason why we're so good at what we do.'

'Taking pictures with a camera from the 1970s is the reason why you're good at what you do?'

'No, it's how we show what we do, authentically, and how we work, authentically. It's important to have standards to uphold.'

I didn't say anything else because I couldn't bear to hear the word authentic one more time. At first, I laughed, but after the third time, when I realized he was authentically saying authentic, I tried to limit the conversation as much as possible. Turns out, on a four-hour drive, that's pretty damn hard when someone from a faraway land wants to prove he is an expert of this land to the driver, Olivier, and the local fixer, Desmonde, who both happen to have been born in and, to the best of my knowledge, never left said land.

The classroom floor was concrete and the shattered windows had metal bars over them to keep the larger animals out. Though a wasp drifted through. It was the most menacing creature I'd ever seen: a head the size of a peanut, wings as big as a hummingbird's, and a long, thin spine connected to a stinger larger than an X-Acto knife. It caused a commotion in the classroom, which I imagined happened often, but the wasp soon drifted out the opposite window and all was settled.

Wooden desks meant for two sat four students, crammed like a pack of unopened cigarettes praying for an addict. The tin roof rustled with a light wind and baked under the sun, turning the classroom into an oven. The teacher stood in front of a chalkboard and instructed the students to smile as they recited from their books, books that the Firm had produced for them, using the Firm's own curricular expertise for what level these students should be at, judging by their age and no other factors.

Sweat ran down the students' faces as they baked in the classroom with their ripe bodily odors. They smiled. It seemed they were taught to do so whenever a camera was around. Maybe the kids knew that smiling showed they were happy, and that this place wasn't what the media had told the rest of the world it was, and they had an even deeper understanding of how to market themselves. Or maybe they were motivated by the voluntourists who passed through with their own cameras, taking photographs in exchange for coins they'd toss to the children. Did they expect us to toss coins at them? I didn't have any change or local currency. Whatever the reason, they knew how to perform in front of the camera and that made my job easier.

I had never taken pictures of children before. Well, there was the odd family photo that I was contracted to do, but I tried to stay away from those. There was money in it, yes, especially in target-rich Washington, DC; young families with young aspirations, hoping to change the world. I captured their naïveté on camera. The trade-off was no artistic freedom, nothing to photograph except posed mothers and fathers trying to keep their faces smiling while their kids squirmed.

Since drifting away from family portraits, I'd moved toward product shoots: promotions for local bars, food porn shots for restaurants, and online shopping gizmos: social media was a black market for anything and everything. Once, I'd taken photos of a clamp that removed tea bags from tea, claiming to drain the bag of water without causing a spill. I didn't ask the company if they'd used a spoon before.

One of the guys on the tea clamp marketing team, after chatting about photography, asked me if I'd ever shot with film before. I told him not since the noughties. If I wanted to get back into it, as an expert amateur himself, he suggested a camera store downtown, run by a cranky widower with a cane – his words, not mine – called Richard.

I found Richard to be quite the charmer; it seemed he wanted someone to talk to. He'd had enough of the kids coming in, buying film for the fad, and then returning to sell back the cameras they'd purchased not a month earlier. His store was the size of a closet, maybe even a little smaller. I don't know how he fit in all that gear. Rows of film cameras and lenses lined within a glass case papered one side of the store, while the other side was covered with flyers for photography classes and gallery showings from the past several decades. Below the glass case was a graveyard of camera cases and bags. There was dust everywhere, including on Richard's rimless glasses. He had soft wrinkles on his face and his belly protruded over the top of the counter. A lone photograph of a woman reclining on a green chaise lounge in her living room smiled at the camera from a frame on the wall behind him. It was a picture of his wife, from a few years before she'd died. I let him tell me about her, between talking about photography and the changing landscape of the art; in his opinion, it had become too pixilated. In the end, he gave me a few free rolls of film for the conversation.

Once I'd walked away with my new old film camera, I used all of the 'film is not dead' hashtags, posted a picture of my vintage camera and film negatives, to let people know I was hip. A college buddy of mine, who happened to see my posts, worked for this Firm that needed a photographer to travel and take some pictures of their products. Another marketing gig, with travel? Count me in.

This was also my first contract shooting film. I was familiar with the medium's intricacies but had never used it on a job; digital processed quicker, sharper, and was much less expensive. Thousands of photos can be stored on a reusable memory card. A typical roll of film has thirty-six shots and, once expended, it's gone. Thankfully, the Firm said they'd pay the costs, but unfortunately there's no price tag on the chemical-induced headache of processing, or the smell staining not only my clothes but my skin, seeping into my pores. But, when a contractor offers what they did, how could I say no?

When the firm and I were discussing what I'd be taking pictures of, I had to explain to them that, no, I had never done this type of shooting before and so was unaware of the ethics and would like them explained to me. I think it's immoral to take photos of people without their permission, and possibly illegal for marketing purposes, and of kids without their parents' permission. The company explained that they were working with the Ministry of Something or Other in the Country and they had jurisdiction,

jurisdiction that allowed them to take photographs to promote the good that their work was doing, in the hopes of increasing donations.

'So, the Ministry of Something or Other can just give us blanket permission to take pictures of kids at school? Without their parents knowing?'

Ron seemed puzzled by my question, as if the answer was obvious, that of course, for the good of the work the Firm was doing, the cost of parental permission and exploitation was worth the overall benefit. He explained that they had several projects running across several countries in several sectors, and that I was expected to take photographs of all of these 'initiatives,' as he called them. Not all at once, mind you, but this trip was the first one. My expectations were uncertain.

I guess the advantage to shooting film is in the mechanics. From the Capital of the Country, we had taken the long ride, over muddied dirt roads in Land Cruisers, to get to the school where I would take pictures of the children. Though it was sunny and clear now, it was the rainy season in the Country and a downpour could come out of nowhere. If any of that wetness penetrated the digital camera, I'd be stuck soaking it in rice for at least a day. Now, I wouldn't go out of my way to drench the strictly mechanical nature of this old-school 35mm SLR, but it could take a beating. Maybe the film would get ruined, but wipe the camera off, load a dry roll, and I'd be good to go. Can't damage the electronics if there aren't any.

The expected rain came halfway through the shoot. I instructed Desmonde, who translated to the teacher who instructed the children, on how to pose, where to place their fingers on the page, and how to look at the camera. One of the kids looked at me as if he couldn't comprehend my existence, why I was there with this film camera, taking pictures of him, so far from my own home. I didn't exactly blame him, in fact, I admired him. But I had a job to do, so we swapped him out with a girl who hadn't stopped smiling since we walked in the door.

As we worked, the soft patter of rain began to sound on the tin roof. Desmonde put his hands up, 'Guess that means it's time to have a break.'

'What? Why?'

My question was soon answered by the suffocating downpour that drowned out any hope of hearing or being heard. Add to that the elation of the children whose lesson was now on hold and the screams of joy that followed, I'm surprised I didn't lose my hearing.

Ron, Desmonde, and I went outside and stood under a small overhang. Olivier sat in the car with his feet on the dash and his hat over his eyes.

Puddles pooled around the Land Cruiser; the thick mud turned soupy as the blue day turned gray.

'Why'd we travel here during the rainy season?' I asked.

'It fit with our project schedule,' Ron said.

Desmonde pulled out a pack of cigarettes and offered them to Ron and me. Ron declined but I took one. He handed me a lighter and I inhaled.

'The rain drowns out the smell of the classroom. Brings in a fresh wind,' said Desmonde.

I thanked him for that bit of knowledge, 'So does the smoke.'

As we stood there and waited for the downpour to end, I saw a goat tied to the end of a wooden stake in the field outside the school grounds. It looked neither perturbed nor content but resigned. Maybe the goat was content. It had a thick belly, more than enough fat to keep warm. Whatever it felt, its feet were stuck in the mud.

ARIANE PARRY

Ariane Parry is a fiction writer, poet, and filmmaker from Penarth in South Wales. Her writing has been published in *Lighthouse*, *adjacent pineapple*, and others, and she is a 2018 Funny Women Short Film Awards finalist for her script, 'Any Time / Any Place'.

www.arianeparry.com
arianeparry@hotmail.com

A Comedian
An excerpt from a novel

The bus windows were so thick with condensation that the passengers couldn't see the city outside. Kay's stomach was empty and she wasn't familiar with the route. She spent the journey conscientiously wiping moisture from that window in case someone else needed the view to identify their stop. Most passengers Kay assumed were seasoned commuters, knowing when to alight because they had memorised the journey by its beats. Her armpits were damp and as more people entered the bus, she felt her neck and collarbones pulse with the same soggy feeling. It was clammy but uncomfortably warm.

Kay's recent open mic hadn't been as successful as her first. She still valued that feeling of control and relief at being able to right herself if something went wrong. She had five minutes of jokes she could recite and a few others she could fall back on if her better material didn't gel. At that last performance, she'd realised that her act lacked an ending. After her last joke, she gave an awkward smile, walked off the stage and asked her friends 'was that OK?' The enthusiasm in their response was quieter than the first time she'd performed.

There was another sense of disappointment that her onstage persona was just a variation on her actual self. The powerful new feeling at her first gig had not transformed her, internally or externally. Telling jokes she had written herself felt like a trap – the limits of her imagination would soon be exposed. Every time she became comfortable making one choice over another, she would suddenly feel a huge temptation to go in the opposite direction.

After her performance, Stewart had shown her a photo he'd taken of her when she was onstage. Looking at the picture was satisfying but painful. Here was the proof that she'd done this thing. Her facial expression and grip on the microphone suggested confidence. It could have been a photo of a much more experienced comedian. The phrase entered her head – *like a real person*. But her nose was not as small as she generally felt it should be. She'd chosen an outfit that she thought was casual, but in the photo it looked sloppy. Her shoulders were hunched and her oily forehead caught the light. It was hard to identify why she felt this way, but she was sure the picture didn't resemble her. She smiled and thanked Stewart for taking it.

When she arrived and the café was empty she was flooded with fear that she was at the wrong venue. She asked the girl arranging glasses behind the bar.
   'The meeting is downstairs, in the cellar.'
   'Oh cool, and do I pay you now?'
   'No, you can pay Jo. I think she's already down there.'
   'Great.' Kay heard her stomach rumble.
   From the stairwell she could hear the scrape and creak of furniture being dragged around, lifted, and set down again. The cellar had whitewashed walls and a raw cement floor which sounded aggressive against the wooden chairs. Three women were dragging the chairs out from a dark corridor that ran underneath the café's kitchen. The chairs were being arranged in an oval. There was a gap at one narrow end of the oval which must have constituted the stage – it wasn't raised, but it was flanked by speakers. The oldest of the three women stood there in olive dungarees and a sunshine-coloured jumper, frowning as she mumbled into the microphone.
   'Does this sound right to you?' she asked. It was a question for anyone to answer and one of the others – holding three stacked chairs aloft, with visibly damp underarms – frowned in reply. She dropped her chairs roughly and Kay winced at the clatter.
   'Bit much feedback.'
   'Yes, it's a bit dodgy.' The look of displeasure that she'd given the microphone was thin and when she saw Kay, it quickly lifted in favour of warm extraversion and pride in her setting. 'Hallo, I'm Jo.'
   Kay gave her the five-pound note that she'd warmed in her pocket and was about to mention that she recognised Jo and had seen her act and enjoyed it, when two other women entered the room. Their footsteps down the staircase had been hidden by the continuing din of furniture being arranged. Kay recognised the shorter of the two as a passenger from the fogged-up bus. She was wearing a trench coat over a dress with a puffy skirt and rain still dripped from her hems. When she saw Jo, her eyes widened.
   'The hair looks *great*!' Jo ran a hand over her cropped hair as if she was trying to find a strand that was long enough to tuck behind her ears.
   'Oh, cheers!' There was a different shade of pleasure on her face now. 'Unfortunately, I had the pictures for my Edinburgh show done two weeks ago, so I've got the long hair in all of those!' She gave an eye-roll with a smile.

'I bet they look fab.'

The room gradually filled with women, some who placidly sat in the first empty chair they found to wait for the event to begin, others who headed directly for familiar faces, their arms wide for hugs. No one sat next to Kay, so she took a foil-wrapped sandwich from her backpack, tearing it into pieces that she stuffed into her mouth from the side, as if she could disguise the fact that she was eating at all.

Several of Kay's friends had insisted she come along to tonight's event – a group for women in comedy where participants could hone their craft and get to know each other. Alice had suggested that she'd come along too before eventually backing out, citing exhaustion from work. Kay sat and waited for someone to talk to her, hoping that eating didn't make her look unavailable.

The room was half-full when a grey-haired woman entered with a Starbucks cup in one hand and an expensive-looking leather bag slung over the opposite shoulder. She surveyed the room as she walked and took a seat right next to Jo. Kay watched the two of them speak quickly and was reminded of old films where two people share a closed off compartment in a train.

A blonde woman sat next to Kay and introduced herself.

'I love these nights. Jo's a genius.' She gave a small wave to Jo, who stood up to speak, introducing the group and expressing her excitement for Edinburgh.

'I'm pleased to announce that the leader of today's masterclass is author, comedian and *superstar*, Helen Drake. She's going to talk to us about how to find what's unique about ourselves as comedians.'

A polite round of applause welcomed Helen, with a few joyful whoops. Kay wasn't familiar with Helen's work, but the atmosphere in the room was rising.

'Should I stand?' Helen asked Jo.

'You don't have to.'

'OK, good. Right then. I'm Helen. I've performed my stand-up in probably every city in the UK. I've written three books – two memoirs and a novel. I qualified as a medical doctor at the University of Warwick, though I no longer practise medicine. Religiously, I identify as pagan and I participate in a small coven just outside of the city in a village called Cartwater. I've been married twice and I have three sons.' She took a slow sip of her coffee. 'When you meet people in the industry, you need to be able to explain your act very quickly and with concision. They need to have an immediate idea of who you are and what makes you special. You need that one line about yourself. When I'm introducing myself, I tell people: I'm a comedian, I'm a writer, and I'm a chirologist.'

An echo of confusion circled the room. One voice rose from the crowd: 'What does that mean?'

'Exactly.' Helen leant back and folded her arms. 'That's the hook. Now you're engaged with my story. You want more.' The murmuring continued. The question about chirology wouldn't get an answer. Helen went on.

'Today, you're all going to write a logline for your act. Summarise yourself in a sentence. Who wants to go first?'

'Should we split into smaller groups?' Jo asked. But someone had already raised her hand to volunteer, one of the older women in the room, with long hair in loose ringlets and a cardigan sliding off her shoulders.

'I'm a badass granny,' she began. An appreciative giggle went around the circle. 'I'm quirky—'

'Never call yourself quirky,' Helen snapped.

'OK. I'm a badass young gran, a manic dancer and a...' She shook her head like an Etch A Sketch to refresh herself. 'I'm a secret granny, recovering from addiction with a bit of help from my amazing grandkids and my erotic book group.'

'Brilliant. *Now* I want to hear that story.' The discussion continued around the circle. An average mum was finding the absurdity in suburbia. A girl with red hair was a ballroom dancing champion studying a PhD in microbiology. A closet goth had tried literally every dating app. A Spanish Backstreet Boys fan experienced cultural clashes with her English girlfriend, who preferred NSYNC.

Kay began to wonder if she had enough of an act to summarise. She scraped over the five minutes that she had refined, the jokes she had discarded and the jokes she hadn't finished yet. She calmed herself with the thought that this was, after all, a workshop, and she was there to learn and develop. She was preceded by a Welsh yoga teacher who still hadn't found inner peace and a vegan *Star Trek* fan who had boldly moved out of her native Liverpool mere weeks ago.

'Hi, I'm Kay. I'm a bit nervous now because I'm also from Wales, and I also really like *Star Trek*. Anyway, my act is basically jokes about astrology and coins.' There was a pause. Kay gave a small, tense smile. Helen fixed her eyes on Kay's.

'Are you intimidated by the world?' The room was silent for the first time. The question had stolen the air from Kay's lungs and her brain scrambled to find what it had to do with her act.

'Sometimes, everyone is intimidated by something, sometimes.' Her eyes were wide and her jaw was tight. The question was a non-sequitur and she told herself it would quickly disappear.

'Is it fair to say you're a bit of a nerd?' Jo attempted.

'I'm a nerd? She's the one doing the PhD in microbiology.' A series of gasps and laughs ran around the circle and Kay was immediately embarrassed. 'I mean that in a good way. I mean, you're an expert.' The word 'nerd' was a small animal that had wriggled out of everyone's hands.

'So your act is about collecting coins—'

'I don't collect coins. I have some jokes about coins and how weird it is that the Queen's face is still printed on them.' She looked up, desperately trying to catch the gaze of the person who had previously mentioned writing jokes about pistachios going on dates with pumpkin seeds. It had sounded like the kind of act that Kay wished she could come up with.

'Has that been helpful?' Jo asked, a pleading note in her voice.

'Yeah,' Kay's voice came out crisp and foreign. 'I mean, it's a start.'

'What about you?' Helen asked, turning immediately to the blonde woman on Kay's right.

'I'm a sassy single mum, a Somerset Scorpio, and I sail model boats.'

HELEN RYE

Helen Rye is the 2019/20 Annabel Abbs Scholarship recipient. Her stories have won the Bath Flash Fiction Award, the Reflex Fiction contest, third place in the Bristol Short Story Prize and Manchester Writing School's QMD Prize, appeared in *Best Small Fictions 2020*, and received multiple nominations for the Pushcart Prize.

Helen.rye@gmail.com

Two flash fictions: *The Lost Girls* and *Reel*
Two separate stories from my collection-in-progress

THE LOST GIRLS

The lost girls draw up their stitches at the dying of the month, when the night sky is empty. Thimble and needle eye, together they work, alone in the marsh at the edge of town. Over and under they sew – raw skin and tree bark, heartache and henbane and long strands of hair torn out. They bind and they loom, hawthorn twig to willow stem. Shuttle dip, corncrake feather, rabbit's pelt, bruise. Spin lace-edge of damselflies. Weave it all up till their handiwork lies shimmering between them in the white of their gaze, till it drapes and morphs and takes on the faint cast of a face – a man they know.

    These nights the townsfolk call in their children in fear of the tidal dark pressing their windows; but the bravest go out into the mire in search of the lost girls. Their torches invade the quiet mist, but the lost girls do not want to be found and so they are not found. And the lights move on, loud throats and boot squelch, and the face of the man in the cloth grows clearer as the lost girls weave and stitch, over and under, the things that are torn in each of them.

    And they do want to find him.

    He is smooth skin and promises, he is silk tongue and sweetness; he is the hand that grips her arm and the drink she didn't ask for and sleight of hand and *fizz* and waking up bruised and confused in an alley down the side of the market. He is *this is how you pay for dinner*, and *why else did you wear that unless*, and *I know girls like you, I know what you want*.

    And they know him.

    The town is a patchwork to them. They know every dark stitch and cross-grained sidestreet; they feel in their seamstress bones each house where each human heart lies. And their minds wander, long fingered, till they find this man out, feel the hum and plush of the place where he sits, alone. For now.

    And the lost girls rise up and they surge along topstitch and blackwork, down the curves of the ditch seams where they once walked. They pluck him from his armchair, the velvet grey. They snap threads and rip back-stitches, take sharp little scissors to the knot of him, snip-snip and pull, till the last of what anchors him into this world is severed; draw him free and away, back to where damaged things lie wove in his likeness, in the ribcage shelter of bog oak and reeds.

They hang up their cloth in the marsh-dank, from the branch of a thousand-year skeleton that once was tree. Backwards and forwards it sways on the night breeze. They tilt their heads till they see where to pin him. Tack him into the weft, a tiny motif. Whipstitch him neatly with hamstring and splinter – over and under, over and under, over and under, around and around.

REEL

Catriona plays the squeezebox in the backroom bar, and it breathes for her when the air deserts her lungs. The men dance, stamping and stumbling, women the same, arms high, a drink spun spilling here; everybody laughing, and Geoffrey the most – she looks away from his face flung back, though it never turns her way. His mouth's wide, shouting at the ceiling, wide enough to swallow her whole.

Breathe in, breathe out, turn the chorus to the bridge and on.

The shake and pound of the floorboards jars the bones of her, throbs the veins in her head, but her fingers know the body of the accordion like they know her own body, how to make each sing, like they know Geoffrey's.

Breathe.

The familiar of the keys – warm bone and blackwood, the firesmoke sting – these are both a comfort and a dragging fishhook to her heart as they recall her, eyes shut, to her grandfather's hearth. The years-old instrument weighting her – *put to memory the melodies, rhythms winding, over and over, feel the beat, the breath of them, let them into your blood, your legs too short to reach the stone flags as you keep time with your Sunday shoes.* Fenland peat smouldering. Geoffrey in the visitor's chair – always Geoffrey wherever she looks, then and now – serious chin pressed into the violin rest, the unmoving focus of his eyes on some point she can't see, beyond the black-pin gaze of the crows and songbirds stretched skin and feather over wire by the old man who looked into the flames and far away from them, who beat his stick on the floor, *one, two, three, breathe*. Geoffrey in the old farm barn when they were seventeen, skin slick and wanting.

Geoffrey here and now and dancing.

Breathe.

And the second chorus draws them all into one together in the gaslit bar, and there's no need to look – she can feel the heave and spin of bodies. She can feel Mary-Anne fly past light, thick hair swinging like a bird alive itself, heel and toe, Mary-Anne's breath in the room, the moon-strong draw of her. She knows which way Geoffrey's eyes are tilted now, same as every time she's seen him since Mary-Anne first took her place in the Sunday pew last spring, him and every other village man, since his letters to Catriona shortened and faltered and stopped.

And the strength of her arms wanes till she fears they'll not carry the lilting triplets of the dance through the silence of her own chest. But in the wheeze of the accordion, her grandfather's voice sings to her of courage. Tells her again that life is no fairy tale; that there are things you want that you never can have – voice of the man who cradled six babies and saw but one grow, whose wartime took his thighbone and his livelihood and everything except the *one-two-three* of this.

Sings that rhythm can carry you through anything, if you'll only *breathe*.

TWISHAA TANDON

Twishaa Tandon has a BA in Sociology from Delhi University. She has worked as a social campaigner in Delhi and her work can be found in Indian publications such as *The Quint*, *The Citizen* and *Youth Ki Awaaz*. Her short story 'Amoli' was selected for the semi-finals of The Halifax Ranch Fiction Prize.

twishaa244@gmail.com

Mirabai
An extract from a novel

What's that in your hand, soldier? A cask, yes. What is this cask made of? I see you frown. If the substance in your cask was not wine, you would've spat on the ground to make your displeasure known. But now you gulp it down. Grudgingly. It's the last you have left and there's nowhere you'll find a refill in Lord Krishna's home.

You wish you were elsewhere. Some place where you could close your eyes and inhale the vapours of the wine, let it course through your blood; let your mind float weightless in music and merriment. Even an expedition to fight the mighty badshah in Delhi would've been better. At least then, you wouldn't be forced to sit and listen to a woman. The only women there would've been from your fantasies. Bending to every will, fulfilling every desire. Not this woman, me, sitting here on this raised platform, commanding the attention of enough people to raise doubts about my authority.

It's not all bad though, soldier. Who would you rather hear this story from? A pandit? He who has been trained in the scriptures, who knows the thoughts of gods, has the authority, the necessary gravitas for such a tale? But I'll tell you why it is better to hear it from me. Try drinking from that cask in front of a pandit telling you a story. Even if a red ant bit you on your back, you wouldn't move. Then having been in the presence of someone so holy and so pure, you wouldn't dare use your fingers to relieve the itch even in the privacy of your home. You would've procured a staghorn, if not from your storehouse, your neighbour's, to scratch away the itch.

This isn't so bad, then. You can drink. You can sneeze. You can scoff. You can shut this down for I am a mere woman. Not even the princess or saint – however you choose to identify her – you're here to take away with you. I'm telling a story at an inappropriate time in an inappropriate place to an inappropriate audience.

I know you will not answer my question about your cask, and I will no longer ask you to stoop so low. This question does not require special expertise. We all know it is made of leather. That horse tied to the tree, is it yours? Persian breed, armoured, prepared for battle, but the sword, look at the sword, it should've been on your person. Instead, it is strapped below the saddle. You're a proper soldier, prepared for battle, but you also come in peace. Or have I got it the other way around? You come here in peace but are prepared for battle. You say Mirabai is still your queen. You say you need her back in your palace for the peace of Mewar, and you're prepared to *fight* for this peace if you need to. An abduction to end all abductions. A fight to end all fights. A battle to end all battles.

Now, this is not so different from the story of Ilyaz Khan, who had been on one such quest as he trudged through Jaisalmer's golden sands in search of refuge. This was before Mira was born. Sultan Bahlul Lodi was sitting on the throne of Delhi. Ilyaz arrived at a makeshift caravanserai. Just one tent, gleaming white in the darkness, with two torches marking its entrance. Ilyaz could see the shadow of a guard dozing off on his stool, his elbow slipping from his thigh. Did he expect more? Rao Dudaji, our beloved Mira's grandfather, had patted him on the back and said, 'Have faith, friend! Have faith. You concentrate on the task at hand and leave the rest to us.' But even though his voice exuded confidence and the grip of his hand was reassuring, Ilyaz knew that Rajput arrangements would be no match for his former master, the sultan.

Ilyaz Khan knew he would find himself in one of the Rajput courts sooner or later. He had waited and waited for the sultan to notice him, as long as any loyal servant could if he had already proven himself not only on the battlefield but also in matters of business. Bahlul Lodi's ascension to the throne was fraught with difficulties, with some still loyal to the abdicated sultan, but Ilyaz had managed a peaceful transfer of all previous goodwill, including trade links with the Afghans. This meant the sultan was able to import his prized horses from Persia, which galloped and captured kingdoms right from the Hindu-Kush mountains to nearly Ganga's delta in Bengal, and through it all, the years and years spent warring, Ilyaz had kept up a steady flow of dry fruits for the sultan's beloved mutton dishes and homesick craftsmen that kept alive the memory of his village.

The sultan always said he loved Ilyaz Khan. He trusted him like his own. But it was only *like* his own because those who were really his own, his nephews, Raza and Himaqat, had been given the portfolios of war and trade and grand palaces of their own, with little responsibility. The sultan's nephews hadn't so much as glanced at an accounts book in their lives. 'Seven camels for our friends from Kabul as promised and throw in two more as a symbol of our love!' A large brotherly embrace and three drinks later, their large pink mouths would add more to their pot of love – three elephants, the revenue of two districts, sacks of Kashmiri saffron and a train of silk long enough to wrap the palace in. Ilyaz Khan was left to go back on all the promises made the previous night, suffer the rancid smell of Kabuli wine on their breaths next morning, or worse, their dazed incomprehension. He'd leave a note for them to read when they returned to their senses. It would tell them the king values their friendship, welcomes them to stay as long as they like (keeping in mind the guest house would need to be vacated for other guests due to arrive for the month of Ramadan, or Eid, or even Diwali or Holi, if those were sooner), and would like to present them with (a much-watered down list of) perhaps two camels and spices to last them a few months.

Ilyaz Khan was tired of this routine. His turban now revealed a shiny bald head, and his beard was grey. The sultan didn't seem in a hurry to change things. He was busy preparing his young son to ascend to the throne. One day, as Ilyaz pulled the strings of his peshwaj together, he saw himself. He saw his large breasts resting on his protruding stomach; large pink nipples; a line of dark fuzzy hair funnelling down from his chest in a semi-circle to his crotch. His wife, Hamida, was buzzing around the room, making the bed, refilling the water jars, when she turned around and found him looking down at himself.

'What are you looking at?' Hamida asked him. 'Don't you have to get to work?' She placed the earthen pot that was in her arms on the floor and went around to help him get dressed.

'How long have I been like this?'

'Been like what?' She pulled the strings together to tie them.

'No, don't tie them. Look at me. How long have I been like this?'

She stood back and placed her hands on her hips. 'Are you seeing your body for the first time, man? I knew this crisis would be upon us sooner or later. Saira said her husband has started asking her odd questions too. *Have you ever really been happy? What would you do if you lived just for yourself?* Absurd!' Hamida pulled the strings with some force and tied the peshwaj. 'Nah, nah, don't wince. I ask you to come out for a walk with me every evening. Every single evening. Come to the king's gardens with me. Let's take a stroll through the bazaars. But no, you have to entertain this official, then that. And now, you look at me, when your drawstrings are nearly running out of length, as if I never told you something that should've been obvious every time you had difficulty turning in your sleep.'

She clothed him, placed the turban on his head, had a final look at his hunched shoulders and dumbstruck face, gave a light pat on his shoulders and moved on.

It was time. Ilyaz was going to alter his fate. Some people achieved glory later in life. Ilyaz felt a restlessness, a quivering in his bones, that told him it was possible for him too, and here he was now, standing before a good-for-nothing tent, before a good-for-nothing guard, who was drunk and asleep. Ilyaz shook him awake.

'Wake up, you lout!'

'Huzoor!' He said, startled, and then his eyes began to droop, and he was asleep again.

'Wake up!' Ilyaz pulled the guard's stool by its leg and flung it away. The guard fell to the floor. He was awake now. Rubbing his back.

'Huzoor?' He asked, standing up, unsteady.

'Ilyaz Khan. You had better have a bed ready, or I swear on Allah, you won't see the light of day.'

The guard's post was separated from the rest of the tent by a thick velvety curtain. There was movement behind it and the sound of stumbling. The curtain parted and a woman emerged. She bent before Ilyaz Khan.

'Huzoor, I'm sorry I can't prostrate. My bad leg refuses to bend to the will of even respected men like you. I have punished my body for years and now, it is punishing me.'

Ilyaz Khan was staring at the woman's legs beneath her skirt. One leg was thrice the size of the other. He looked up at her face. There was a small smile on her lips. Her head was uncovered and her long hair hung loose. She was unlike the Rajput women Ilyaz had seen at Rao Dudaji's palace. They rarely came to court. He only caught glimpses of them through the intricate stone lattice above the floor of the court. Never any faces; just their glittering nose rings and bangles.

'What's your name?'

'For you, Shakeela, huzoor.'

'For me?'

'Doesn't matter, huzoor. Consider me one of your own. I'll take care of you tonight. Before Hukum Singh went on his evening binge, he told me you were stopping by for just one night. Is that correct? If longer, we can make arrangements.'

'Inshallah I'll leave tomorrow.'

'I have the bed ready for you.' She drew back the curtain. There wasn't much. It was nothing in comparison to the caravanserais he was used to. They had large gardens, and the ones closer to cities like Delhi, Multan and Kabul even had fountains. They were equipped with large troughs of grass and water canters for the horses. The rooms were like any in a palace, luxurious with Persian rugs and soft silk pillowcases. This, though spare, with only a bed, a sheet stretched to its limit across the bed and one bolster, was neat and enough for Ilyaz, who had spent the last week in the wilderness. There was a lamp on one side of the bed that lit an earthen pot lying next to it. There were other tiny bundles on the other side of the room that Ilyaz wasn't bothered to explore.

ROSE VAN ORDEN

Rose Van Orden studied History and German at Oxford University before spending 17 years as a strategist in advertising agencies and at the BBC. *Chimera Forever*, her first novel, throws its heroine, approaching forty, into the different versions of her life had she stayed with each of her loves.

rose.vanorden@googlemail.com

Chimera Forever
An extract from a novel

The water of the swimming pool wobbles like unset jelly. A crocodile with cartoon eyes quivers on its surface. The heat holds everything else as if in amber: the terracotta town of Siena way down below, rooftops packed tightly together. My sister Tara on the lounger next to mine, her skin sleek from suntan lotion.

My fingers hold a small tile bearing the letter *R*.

'Please just go,' says Tara, eyes closed behind her sunglasses.

We're about ten goes in, and the Scrabble board has taken on a fixed quality.

'How many possible combinations do you reckon there are?' I say, playing for time. 'How many different versions of the game?'

Tara breathes in deeply through her nose. This exact form of tedium is what she hates about Scrabble.

'You're the strategist,' she says.

'Must be nearly infinite possibilities,' I say, although my run of consonants suggests few. I place the *R* after an *O*.

'Is that it?' says Tara, turning onto her side to peer at the board. She rearranges the tiles on her rack. 'Of course the possibilities aren't infinite. There's only a set number of letters.'

She transports tile after tile onto the board.

'And in this particular version of the game, I'm out.' She lies back, a pleased-with-herself smile on her face. She might be able to spell it, but I bet she doesn't even know what *JACQUARD* is.

I reach behind me to release the top of the lounger, lay it flat and turn onto my front. I place my chin on my hands and close my eyes, the scent of chlorine mixed with Nivea. The hum of crickets all around swells and then falls. In the distance, the bell of the Duomo tolls. I turn over, pull up the top of the lounger, clip it into position. Maybe I should get into the pool.

I shouldn't have had that coffee. There must be a word for it – for the restlessness brought on by a double espresso after lunch. The Italians must call it something. Lizzie would know, but she's up at the house with

Maximilian and the children and Fred – Tara's wholesome boyfriend – and our parents. Perhaps I'm gripped by a deeper impatience. Because it's September and summer holidays are meant to be in August and life is moving on, but we're still here, on pause. Or because it's the eleventh year we've come to this house and each year's fortnight blends into one, the memories forming a montage as if it was all one long holiday, and the only thing that changes is that more people are added. Although I haven't added anyone.

I pick up *Gente* magazine from the ground. The heat and our sun-creamed hands have made it sticky; the coloured ink comes off on my fingers and my belly. I flick from the back – photos of people on holiday, famous only in Italy. I soon reach the front cover, where a man with dark hair and strong arms smiles at us. He's not wearing a shirt; he's all skin, the sky is blue behind him, and collapsed against his bare chest, beaming, is a thrilled woman. A different life, the life where I'm the woman in the man's arms, assumes its position in my mind with such clarity, such entitlement, that it's impossible not to believe that one day I'll touch it, experience it for real.

'I want someone who makes me feel like that,' I say, holding the magazine over Tara's face, prodding her until she takes it from me.

'Really?' she says, handing back the magazine. 'I think you'd get bored. Anyway, he looks just like David. Or *Game of Thrones* guy.'

'Sebastian? He had ginger hair.'

'An Italian version of Sebastian.'

I put down the magazine, lie back.

'We didn't finish talking about your birthday party,' says Tara.

'I don't even know if I want a party anymore.'

'It's your fortieth – you have to have a party!'

'I wish I had someone to help me.'

'I'm helping you.'

'I mean my special person.'

Tara turns her head towards me, and she doesn't need to say anything because we both know what she's thinking. There's encouragement there though, I can feel it.

'If I had the chance again,' I say, 'I'd be... I don't know. Less impulsive? In retrospect, none of my relationships needed to end.'

'Just one,' says Tara, 'You only need one not to end.'

A squawk of laughter, and they're upon us.

'Auntie Franny! Auntie Tara!' they shout.

Tara and I do not move, savour these last horizontal moments, the sun's heat so intense it's pulsing.

'Mummy said you'd swim with us,' announces Margot as the children line up at the foot of our loungers. Minnie, with her halo of pale curls, wears a polystyrene vest and rubber ring. Merlin wears Speedos and orange armbands. He gazes absent-mindedly at my boobs. Margot, disconcertingly, wears nothing that will float.

'Hello, you chaps,' says Tara, lifting only her head, just as Merlin turns, runs the few paces to the pool and bombs in. The splash rains cold on our legs. Margot whoops and takes a running leap onto the blow-up crocodile; she slides straight off. Minnie waddles to the pool edge, flaps her arms and jumps.

'It's your moment,' says Tara. 'Thank goodness for your lifeguard training.'

'Why are you such a dick?' I say, springing to my feet, scanning the pool.

Minnie surfaces like a bobbing apple, grins open-mouthed and close-eyed, her hair stuck to her face. Merlin has made it to the shallow end, where he stands, occupied with something. Margot breast-strokes towards him, asserting her authority with every dip and rise of her head. Tara catwalks along the hot flagstones in her string bikini and Ray-Ban aviators. Arms crossed, she peers down upon Margot and Merlin.

'Don't touch it,' she suggests. 'OK, put it on the edge. Frances?'

I slide into the water to commandeer Minnie in her ring.

Merlin turns to us with his treasure: a dead frog, white and bloated, splayed on his small hands. Minnie wants to touch it; I cover her hand with mine.

'I'm going to get Fred,' says Tara.

'Great,' I say.

'Why's it not moving?' Merlin's German accent is stronger with the emotion of the find.

'It's dead,' I say.

'It might just be sleeping,' says Margot.

'I'm afraid it's not going to wake up,' I say.

'Why not?'

'Because it's not meant to swim in chlorine.'

'Why not?'

'Because chlorine isn't natural, it doesn't give the frog what it needs.'

'How come it's OK for us to swim in?' demands Margot. 'Is chlorine poisonous?' In German she mutters to her brother to get rid of the frog and get out of the pool. It's not safe. With a grunt, Merlin hurls the frog as far as he can, it hang-glides towards Siena. Minnie begins to wail.

CHIMERA FOREVER – 167

'Let's go!' instructs Margot and although the water is shallow enough for a six-year-old to walk in, she swims to the ladder, holding her chin above the water. Merlin levers himself out of the pool, his bottom tiny in his tight trunks.

'Mummy!' shouts Margot once on dry land, 'Mummy!'

And although we can see no one from where we are, a mother's supersonic hearing sends Lizzie down the slope towards us, arms out for balance, her kaftan fluttering as she runs. 'What's happened?' She calls, frantic. 'What's happened?' She gasps as she reaches us. 'What's happened?'

I'm still in the water, my hands on the rungs of the ladder, arms safely sandwiching Minnie in her ring. Upon seeing her mother, Minnie's wail crescendos. Merlin joins in. Lizzie swoops and lifts Minnie from the water, her small feet almost hitting my face. She kneels to examine her. I am invisible and a bad person somehow. Margot raises her voice to give her account over the din.

On the way to my room, I pass Tara and Fred, in their own little world on the narrow bench under the olive tree. A note is wedged into the windowpane of the back door: 'At Carrefour! M & D XXX'

The house is dark and cool as a wine cellar. It takes a moment to adjust to the dim light. I walk through the kitchen and past the heavy wooden dining table that we never use. A dumping ground for leaflets picked up in Siena churches, half-full bottles of San Pellegrino, a pair of cheap sunglasses from the farmacia.

Upstairs I flop onto my bed. I shut my eyes, a sharp sting of chlorine. My post-caffeine brain falls in on itself.

I open my eyes to find Margot at my bedside and immediately feel horribly louche. She's dressed, her washed hair slick with comb tracks.

'Hi, Margot,' I say. 'I'm about to have a shower.'

'But you were asleep.'

'I was resting my eyes.'

'Do you want to use our shower?'

'I have my own bathroom.'

'You only have a bath.'

'When I said shower, I meant bath. There's a showerhead thing, I can...'

We're both in the small bathroom now, the floor tiles cold against my feet. I do my mirror face, pouting as I pull out the hair elastic before leaning in to inspect the freckles that have appeared on my nose. The words sun damage bounce in my mind, and I wish we didn't all know so much, wish there were things we could just enjoy, like having a tan.

'Auntie Franny?' says Margot. 'Do you have my make-up?'

'Let me see.' I unzip my make-up bag and find the little pink pot, round with a domed lid, that Margot has had a thing for since she was two years old. Strange, how she doesn't remember living in America – as she and Lizzie and Max did then – when she was so alive at the time, knew the names of every neighbour, would call 'Hi, Maurice' all the way down the street, never got a name wrong. Doesn't remember any of it now. But she remembers the little pink pot. She opens it, plucks out the curved brush nestling inside, swirls it in the powder and brushes it onto her cheeks. Margot is fair, it doesn't take much blusher to make her cheeks pink, but the light in the bathroom is dim and she keeps swirling and brushing and by the time the bath has run she's given herself sunburn.

Satisfied, she places the pot back where it belongs. I dip my hand into the water to check the temperature and turn off the tap.

'Franny,' says Margot, 'Do you have a best friend that you can marry?' She turns her toe on the bathroom floor. 'Do you have a boyfriend or girl-friend that you can marry?'

'It's a good question.'

We smile at each other.

'What about Finn?'

'Finn and I...' I look at the ceiling, the white paint flaking from condensation. 'We're not best friends anymore.'

'Why not?'

'It's just the way it turned out.'

'Why?'

'Sometimes two people can really love each other, but it still isn't enough.'

'Why?'

'I guess we all have different ideas about how we want our life to be, and...'

'I want to be happy,' says Margot, shrugging her shoulders.

'Exactly. We all do.' I'm standing with hand on hip and one leg bent, as if I was the one offering counsel here. From the landing, Lizzie calls the children for their supper.

'See you later, Franny.' Margot sidles away.

I shut the bathroom door, and finally, I'm in my most familiar state: by myself, with only my endless possibilities for company.

ALASTAIR WONG

Alastair Wong employs fictionalised selves in order to dramatise encounters with memory and reflect on his subjective experience, often juxtaposing images with text to explore their interactions. He got a first in English from the University of Oxford and will be attending the Prose Fiction MFA at Brooklyn College, where he received the Truman Capote Fellowship.

ali_wong@hotmail.co.uk

Gesamtkunstwerk; Total Work of Art
An extract from a short story

TOKYO DISNEYSEA

I knew I was feeling real blue when even the jumbo turkey leg didn't do the trick. The meat glistened at me, half-wrapped, several layers of paper all shined through with grease. It tasted smoky and fatty but somehow a little dry and sad too. On such a hot day, why Sis wanted a turkey leg so bad, I couldn't tell you, but I didn't have the heart to argue. Though seeing all these kids skipping around, clutching these prehistoric hunks of meat in their tiny hands like something out of the Flintstones, was actually pretty funny. And so for breakfast, we strolled around eating meat off the bone.

The leg is something of a running joke amongst Disneyphiles, and Disney themselves must be in on it. I saw hats and shirts with the turkey leg on that said 'Nice and Juicy', car air fresheners too. Some clever cookie named Dave Jarrett – a veritable giant in the field of theme park foodstuffs – got the wise idea to start selling them here at a stall called 'Big Al's Coonskin Caps' in the '80s. For the sake of publicity, they even got a guy in a turkey leg costume to race Olympic hurdler David Payne on YouTube. God's own truth. And the rest, as they say, is history.

Disney sell over two million a year. One million turkeys at two legs apiece. But what happens to the rest of the poor turkey anyway? Sis kicked me hard when I asked her this, for putting her off, she said. I imagined one million legless carcasses and felt goosebumps coming on because that was exactly how I saw myself: legless, stuck in the mud.

They were selling Mickey and Minnie ears at the same place, and we bought those too. I was against giving Disney too much business, so Sis said she'd pay. Sis was having a jolly time, and I was going to try my best.

We were both in all black. We were both in leather. We thought the day would be funnier like that: two goths charging around – mouse ears and turkey legs – frightening children and hopefully parents too. After the long trip from Tokyo, might as well make the most of it. We ambled about for a while, admiring the glittering artifice of everything: the fake volcano, the fake trees and plants, the characters in fursuits.

I don't even think I mean fake pejoratively – there *is* something beautiful about being someplace where the worst thing that might happen to you is standing in a long queue. The people were real, mainly families, but people like Sis and me too. And I think the laughter was real, but how can you tell when you're in a cynical mood and don't much know the people laughing? On the internet, a Japanese person types 'wwwww' – the first letter of warau, meaning laughter – instead of 'hahahaha'. So laughter is inflected by language too. I wondered about the accent of their laughter and what mine would sound like to them – had I laughed.

Indiana Jones had a 'single rider' option so, by sitting apart, we skipped most of the queue. Inside the lifesize Temple of Doom, there was something in the air: humid and musty, rather like an attic or standing on a hot subway vent. Kids squeezed their parents' hands, and I tried to remember their excitement and fear; surely, I had experienced it once too.

I am *that* tourist who looks everything up. There is the duty to inform myself, but, to be honest, I feel lost if I do not understand a place. And there were many things I didn't understand, not just about Disney, but about myself. Like why I was blue again and how to tell Sis about it.

Sis said, 'It smells like feet.'

'Oh, I kind of like it.'

We were queuing in a tunnel of sorts, and it frightened me to think that there were workers like rats scurrying below: from my research, I knew about the patented 'utilidors', a system of underground tunnels that connected up the park. Many people want to spend their final day in The Happiest Place on Earth™. Should an accident happen, say, park employees would be able to shuttle the body away with minimal fuss. Poof. Gone. Like magic. To *never* see that happen is part of what you pay for.

In the darkness of the Temple of Doom, I found the space to think. I had been withdrawn of late. That Sis was the only one I shared a language with should have brought us closer together. Instead, we quarrelled over petty things. But it was more than that. Language was a bell jar making me claustrophobic: having no one else to speak to made me self-conscious about my company being good enough.

Still I'll admit it: I got a little excited at the front. The first-time round was a hoot. I did not see the boulder coming. The boulder that charged at us, making everybody scream (do screams have accents too?). We dropped into darkness.

Outside, Sis squeezed my arm. 'Again!'

I feigned reluctance but was secretly glad. The second time, knowing what was coming, the effect moved to a minor key. By the third, nothing; I only wondered if I was having fun yet – if happiness was anything like this. Anticipation and release, up and down, up and down. Sitting with a stranger, sharing a fate, but with no language between us (a curt nod, maybe), now became a special kind of loneliness. I kept my eyes shut.

Somehow by burdening Sis with these nebulous, sappy feelings every single person in DisneySea would bear that brunt too. The ghost of Walter Elias Disney haunted the place with his hand on my shoulder saying not here son, not now. There's a place for that kinda talk, and this sure ain't it. The park was alive; having swallowed me whole, it would regurgitate me, expelling my negativity and my frankly wearying sardonicism. Suck the poison. Spit it out. Barred from Walt's kingdom of heaven. I was all mixed up inside, mixed up like these metaphors... And all this just to say that the idea of making an earnest confession of unhappiness in The Happiest Place on Earth™ seemed perverse and unacceptable; no way to tell if that was all in my head.

The cart jerked to a halt.

'Woooooooo!'

I would recognise that anglophone style of whooping anywhere. I opened my eyes again. The guy next to me was white, my age, early twenties. I caught myself staring, and he looked at me awkwardly, smiling with his mouth shut. A slight bow. He assumed I was Japanese.

NAOSHIMA ISLAND

We dropped our bags off and walked to the new-build onsen out on the seafront. Parting with Sis, I went into the male changing rooms.

My first time at an onsen, I was desperately shy about getting naked. Trying to mask this, I pinned my shoulders back, puffed out my chest and strutted around like the cock of the walk. So badly did I need to take up space. But now I got naked unselfconsciously and locked my things away. There were rows of lonely plastic stools facing fogged mirrors, pink plastic tubs to pour water over your head with. I showered down and made a point of cleaning myself thoroughly, as a sign of respect to the others.

The onsen was open-air with a choice of five pools, varying in temperature and size. It was breezy outside, but that only made the warmth of the spring water more pleasant on my skin. So at ease; as long as I didn't open my mouth, I belonged – was one of them. Swanning between the pools, my stress escaped as steam, wordlessly into the night.

In Tokyo, the perpetual light of neon signs – always somewhere to be and something to do – has replaced all the stars. But here, we were far from any significant light pollution, and it was a beautiful clear night, full of stars. So peaceful you could hear the stately rolling of the waves. From one tall tub with a roof, I could see over the bamboo fence and out onto the long stretch of grey-blue that was the Seto Inland Sea. From another pool, my favourite, I could lie back on a stone pillow and gaze right up at the stars as the warm water glided over me. Unfortunately, no bath offered both views simultaneously: it was not possible to see the sea and the stars together. There was an uncertainty principle at work; I felt a certain pleasure in swapping one partial view for another, the pleasure of continually rediscovering that the other view still indeed existed out *there*.

Here was another space to think. I still hadn't told Sis how I had been feeling. But right then – if not happy – I was, at least, content. I began to believe I was OK, that I wouldn't have to tell her at all. And then I craved, for whatever reason – that turkey leg. How lovely it would be to sit here eating it in the tub! Maybe that's what happiness is to me.

The next day we took our time walking to the Chichu Museum, stopping on sandy beaches that backed onto thick concrete walkways.

Chichu Bijutsukan was built into a hill to avoid disrupting the natural landscape. From a bird's eye view, you would see geometric courtyards – triangles, squares, rectangles – recessed into the ground.

The architect of Chichu, Tadao Ando, once proposed building a green hill, a burial mound, at Ground Zero in New York. The only problem: the site was both mass grave and prime real estate. A bidding war ensued over the rights to redevelopment. The gift shop there – at the 9/11 Museum – has attracted considerable ire; victims' families railing against the sheer crassness of selling baubles and trinkets over the remains. One architect called the commercialisation of the site a 'Disneyfication'. And with grave seriousness Ando said that whatever was built at the site was to become the 'symbolic centre of the world.' I walked around Chichu lamenting the fact that Ando did not get his way.

At Chichu, all exhibits are permanent with only three artists on display: Walter De Maria, James Turrell and Claude Monet. Rather than adapting the work to suit the space, Ando designed a space to house these specific works. There's a rhythm to the experience of moving from artist to artist. Between the rooms he enforced a period of reflection; patiently, I walked through dim corridors before emerging into concrete courtyards, flooded with natural light. Over and over, your mind is wiped clean like an Etch A Sketch.

So as not to damage the marble floor, we had to take our shoes off and put on slippers before entering the Monet room, another sign of respect, making it seem like a holy place. Everything was built to Monet's ideal for looking at his Water Lilies; natural light spills in, coddling the cornerless walls. Seven hundred thousand cubes made up the floor like little dice, faintly streaked with veins. The repetition of the marble cubes stretches out into the infinity of the paintings themselves, lilac and blue. Only by removing your shoes do you realise how miserably the din of repeating footsteps plagues other galleries.

It is difficult to overstate the quality of silence here – different, somehow, to the thinking silence in the Temple of Doom – *this* silence, from an excess of awe, left my mind alive but blank. Awe at the grandeur of the paintings, awe at the artisans who cut the marble and laid each cube by hand, awe at the love (and it is a kind of love) involved in designing a room to communicate one eternal set of paintings. People say we have much to learn from children: entering the room, they became as solemn, as silent, as the adults.

I turned to my sister; she was crying. I did not ask why but felt I understood.

KATHERINE YONG YHAP

Katherine Yong Yhap, having achieved her English Literature and Creative Writing BA at UEA, is now on a similar course at the same place, on the MA. Claiming heritage of her Guyanese, Italian, Chinese, German, Mongolian, Jewish and Amerindian forebears, she hopes her future will be as mixed as her past.

katherineyhap@gmail.com

Tale One

Warm breeze, so close to cool as to make her shiver. In the hollow where Josephus lay is now a squirming mass of tiny limbs. Beautiful Neville, big-headed baby. Still dark, dark out. Her old man will be fishing now. 'Babalo!' Iris calls into the silence, hearing through the thin boards the turning of her daughter's body in bed. A pause, in which her irritation sparks. 'm'Ah come deh.'

The muted voice, heavy with sleep, cuts through Iris's annoyance, but it fails to dissipate. She lies still. The quiet woven through their existence makes music of little bodies sliding and shoving, the tread of light steps. 'Mama?' Iris lifts the infant beside her and hands him to the small girl: 'Clean he.' The door swings closed behind them. Iris rolls over, sighs, sleeps till just before dawn.

—

Leah: named Babalo because she hates it, Puss because she fights like a cat, hefts her bright-eyed little brother through to the room she shares with her new father's children.

Josephus had come with a reputation, the man had money: land, a store. His father was a jungle man, Chinese of course but he lived by his machete like the Amer. No man fought him. Josephus was the same, but smart with money. Hard. She lumps Neville into bed with Errol and Dennis. Errol's eyes pop open, 'Puss! Bai stink!' Fully awake now, the fear of her mother's wrath hitting hard, Leah whips the baby back up and over to the rag pile. Taking two clean squares of rough towelling, she carries the chattering boy across the room and out. Deftly pulling his nappy off, she throws it on the steel drums stacked outside the back door. Awkwardly rinsing him down with the wash jug, Leah grips hard on his fat little arm. The large tin thing belongs on a washstand and is heavy, heavier than Neville and he cries under her pincer grip. It's that or drop to the shitty mud, so she does not relax her hold until he looks clean enough. She moves the sobbing baby to where her hips will be, pours water over the soiled napkin, takes the jug and child back into the house. On the floorboards she shushes him, binds him, carries him back to the bedroom. There is no hatred in her, she likes this child well enough. There is a protection in being his protector. Neville is deposited with his brothers, and Leah slips into the bed she shares with her new sister Lois. They sleep until just before the dawn.

—

A baby's cry ribbons their dreams. Leah stays still. Lois slides from beneath the blanket and sees Neville alone in that big bed, its blanket on the floor. Her high cheek-boned face crinkles in joy that she gets Neville to herself. The grey light drifts like dirty water, but she can see through the thin fabric at the window a glimmer of the day ahead. Lois picks up her littlest brother, kissing him, crooning love words. He clings tight, his strong little fingers with their sharp nails dig in and bring delight, his sobs fade. They dance slowly.

—

Marmar and Bad Monkey sit before the dawn with Dead Suki. Their old bones throb in the morning cool from the open door. Their bed is feather with two blankets each, but in this dusky time of quiet labours, Dead Suki can talk. They know how to honour the lifetime of Dead Suki's twilight planting and harvesting. The only time the living Suki had to doctor and teach her children – make their clothes, lick her own wounds – she stole from sleep. This hour, or two, before the sun rose and she must serve her master: drudge all day, go to his bed at night. They honour her. They sit in their chairs with their free, living bones and they listen. Like all children, they do not always listen well.

Dead Suki's voice comes from within them, whisper-quiet and cracked, but rich as molasses: 'm'Ah picknie. When yuh get old yuh muss get sick. This man a'Iris, he bai picknie never go get sick.'

Marmar nods, her silence a sign of respect. She had never been lashed for speaking out.

'You na know wha' 'bout.' Bad Monkey looks over at Marmar, sly teasing, then to the hearth where Dead Suki's old, old bones have rested for nearly thirty years.

'Yuh t'ink yuh smart? Trini bacoo, yuh – pot hong poohar.' Marmar turns a lazy eye on her old man, her neck an ebony pillar of threat.

'Picong? Star gyal.' Bad Monkey puckers kisses at his woman.

'm'Ah picknie. Too much t'ing me pass tru tuh sit here yuh talkin' nansense...' Dead Suki's voice ghosts away.

'Dead Suki!' Remorseful, Bad Monkey pushes himself from his chair and lights the herb-trunk fire. It is laid, always ready, on the hearth that is Dead Suki's gravestone. Scents of oregano, cinnamon and orange curl up in thin tendrils. He squats, watching the flames grow; lays finger-thick twigs one on one, forming a pyre. Andiroba, cashew. Waiting, nothing, then reverently places slender wedges of cedro heartwood on the sweet fire.

'm'Ah buss yuh backside if yuh na hear me. Picknie come sick a head.' Dead Suki's voice rises hard and bitter.

'When? Who? Mama Suki?' Marmar's voice, high and scared, drops into silence that stretches to the sudden dawn. A cold, hair-thin wail pierces the old couple.

'It went true. It done one bai just now. Mek dat man move a'drums. m'Ah picknie nex.'

Dead Suki's grief floods the house. Whipping grass and scattering jumbees faster than the sun she breaks down the lane, her tide bursting against the screams of the children.

—

Leah pads silently into the pre-day murk which coats the veranda; picking her steps on wood slippy with mud. She takes an armful of sticks and a tinder-dry coconut husk, turns and carries her load in, past the big table, the washpot, stew pots and the rack of knives sharpened to hooks. She stoops at the stove and careful to raise no dust, rakes the ashes through the grate with her fingers. She breaks and lays the hairy husk at the bottom, then the sticks one on one, like Bad Monkey showed her. Leah wants a fat grouper, or a ray; Josephus can fish good – but maybe her brothers managed to shoot a monkey. Maybe Marmar would come after breakfast and clean the monkey good, so she wouldn't get bloody before school. ''Ere.' Lois walks into the room, shielding a lit taper. 'Move nah gyal.'

'T'ank yuh, Lois.' Leah whispers her gratitude. This eldest girl could beat her if she liked, but she knows Lois never would. Lois was so soft as to tempt Leah to beat her, take her money, food and that shop-bought scarf with its fine reds and blues, but she would not. Lois goes to the cellar to fetch the dough, Leah to the well with the big jug. On her way she rinses the napkin again, shitty water slopping to the boards. Sluicing the last of the water to make a clean path to the door she goes on across the yard. A sudden hollering and hands pull her arms, clothes and yank the jug from her hands. The laughter is kind... The boys... A kiss on her hair and Errol runs past her to the house. 'm'Ah got penny butta! Yuh mek feia sista?' Dennis runs past her with three big Fat Snook on a stick, chasing Errol. A fear comes to her with the dawn. In the too bright light Errol darts up the stairs but not on through the door. He turns right, off the sluiced path to the window. He slips. He skids. The world stops and the only thing breathing is Errol. He twists as he cradles the butter, keeping it safe. He laughs loud and slow slow, chin up, he falls. His head hits the edge of a drum with the speed and sound of a gun.

—

Dead Suki got there first. The mist of her impotent love whispering: 'm'Ah na know wha' fuh tell yuh. Me try try. m'Ah picknie.'

Marmar and Bad Monkey race down the path, then Josephus, returned with the sun and made alert by these ancients running like children. Iris stands like a statue in the doorway, cradling her infant, Lois clinging to her skirt. All the children frozen, barely breathing. Tearing their eyes from the corpse of their brother they gaze at their father. Josephus looks to Iris, and then over his silent children, 'Bai na done bleedin. Iris, can wash off butta?'

Iris wants to tell him no, let the boy be buried with his butter. 'Bring priest fust Jo—'

'Hush ya mout.' Josephus pushes his booty of fish and meat in to Marmar's arms. He takes the butter from the dead child and places it on the sluiced path to the door. He tidies Errol's limbs. Bad Monkey appears with an old sheet, and over and over they roll Dead Errol, mud and blood spreading across the whiteness. Silence fills the screaming places in Iris's mind. Her throat closes. She watches.

TALE TWO

Iris sits in her parlour; tightly packed with brown velvet chairs, a black glass coffee table and porcelain figurines. Her five grandchildren lounge with their elbows in, chatter chatter chatter like they don't know fear. Their white, white skin. White the colour of pain. Pretty eyes though, like hers.

All rich dark brown, almond shaped eyes, golden in the sun. Plump full lips. Hair curled like the damned Arete, the other nanny. Iris hates her. She hates Neville's wife too. Skinny little white girl who smiles and nods and runs away. Never comes without Neville anymore. No respect. Disobedient. Ungrateful daughter. Acid churns in Iris's stomach as her mind rages, and her tongue stays still.

'Nanny nanny!' The littlest child beams up at his grandmother, slapping his fat hands on her knees.

'm'Ah pickney,' Iris can't help the warmth, the delight that floods her. This one was whitest of them all, but she had checked his blue spot in the hospital and this bighead baby was her own pickney too. Beautiful like Neville, before that white witch took him from her. Why he stayed away she did not know and now, today, he moves from London, going to where only whites live, North.

Neville has a god; he followed his god. Iris laughed to herself. She picked up and ran from gods like men. They were always men. They were cruel and vengeful and stupid. Men. Her Neville had a god he picked up from her. Those white men and ladies were useful, they had helped find her work and welcomed her to their warm living rooms. They had cars and telephones and Neville was not meant to stay with them, but he did. He married one. His pickney, her pickney were white little boys and girls. She could not hate them. She did not even want to. There was a protection in this white family.

She absently plays with this pickney's jet-black hair, looks up as her son walks into the room.

'Mummy, it's time to go now, it's a long drive. Babalo will come for you next week, she'll bring you to us.' Neville, her big, handsome boy. Tall like his daddy, clever, the first university man she knew. They made him a priest in his church, Elder, they say.

'Mummy?' A clipped, nervous voice cuts across her smile. 'Mummy, thank you for having us. I'll make sure the place is comfortable for you before you come. Come on, you lot.' Her daughter-in-law chivvies the children, who troop over to their grandmother. Some give big hugs and kisses, some mumble and slink out. She grips tight to the bighead pickney, keeping him back to hand to her Neville.

The noise and crowd leave as one, leaving her silent, alone.

ACKNOWLEDGEMENTS

This anthology contains work written by the 2021 cohort of the UEA's MA in Creative Writing: Prose Fiction. We are very grateful for the support of the UEA School of Literature, Drama and Creative Writing, in partnership with Egg Box Publishing, part of UEA Publishing Project, Ltd., without whom this anthology would not have been possible.

We would like to thank our course convenors Philip Langeskov, Naomi Wood, and Tessa McWatt, alongside our other workshop tutors Trezza Azzopardi, Amit Chaudhuri, Andrew Cowan, Julianne Pachico, and Rebecca Stott. We deeply appreciate your invaluable advice and support throughout a challenging year.

Many thanks to the talented author and UEA Prose Fiction alumna, Ayọ̀bámi Adébáyọ̀, who so eloquently considers the highs and lows of studying the course during a pandemic in the foreword to this anthology.

We are thankful to the authors who have contributed to this year's Masterclasses – Eley Williams, Monique Roffey and Sarah Hall – as well as the UEA's International Chair of Creative Writing, Tsitsi Dangarembga.

A huge thank you to Shannon Clinton-Copeland for your guidance and support, and to Emily Benton for the wonderful cover design and typesetting. Thanks also to our hardworking Prose Fiction Editorial Committee: Ope Adedeji, Hannah Cole, Polly Halladay, Michele Lim, Olivia Lowden and Adeola Opeyemi.

Thank you to our attentive and enthusiastic proofreaders: William Bindloss, Laura Cooper, Josephine Henniker-Major, Aidan Maartens, Nathan Merchant, James Mildren, Ariane Parry and Amelia Sparling. We appreciate your help and hard work.

With grateful thanks to the donors who contribute to the scholarships that support our writers, including: the Annabel Abbs Scholarship, the UEA Booker Prize Foundation Scholarship, the Bourne Scholarship, the Curtis Brown Award, the Global Voices Scholarship, the Kowitz Scholarship, the Malcolm Bradbury Memorial Scholarship, the Miles Morland Foundation African Writers' Scholarship, the Novelry Scholarship, the Seth Donaldson Memorial Bursary, the Sonny Mehta Indian Scholarship and Scholarship for Writers, the UEA Crowdfunded Writers' Scholarship.

Finally, thank you to all the students who made up the 2021 cohort. The Covid-19 pandemic shaped the academic year in unimaginable ways, but the value of the friendships made, advice shared, and support offered could never be altered.

UEA MA Creative Writing Anthologies: Prose Fiction

First published by Egg Box Publishing, 2021
Part of the UEA Publishing Project Ltd.

International © retained by individual authors

This book is sold subject to the condition that it shall not, by way of trade or otherwise, be lent, resold, hired out, stored in a retrieval system, or otherwise circulated without the publisher's prior consent in any form of binding or cover other than that in which it is published and without a similar condition including this condition being imposed on the subsequent purchaser.

A CIP record for this book is available from the British Library
Printed and bound in the UK by Imprint Digital

Designed by Emily Benton Book Design
emilybentonbookdesign.co.uk

Proofread by Sarah Gooderson

Distributed by NBN International
10 Thornbury Road
Plymouth
PL6 7PP
+44 (0)1752 202 301
e.cservs@nbninternational.com

ISBN 978-1-913861-25-4